I0745948

The Uncle Tal Stories

<u>Disclaimer:</u>
No character in this story is taken from real life. Any resemblance of a character to any person or persons living or dead is accidental and unintentional. Any resemblance of a commercial trade name to a real-world trademark is likewise accidental and is in no way intended to portray any link to the company holding that trademark. The author, their agents and publishers cannot be held responsible for any claim otherwise and take no responsibility for any such coincidence.

This book written in Palatino Linotype, using Office 365™.
Title font in Papyrus, chapter headings in Quarrystone.

Title: The Uncle Tal Stories
Author: Alan M. Atkinson (1970—)
Subjects: Time Travel, Science Fiction

First Printing: 2025

Printed and distributed by IngramSpark™ (www.ingramspark.com)

ISBN: 978-1-7638780-1-3

Alan M. Atkinson
Words on Paper (Ink)
Townsville, QLD 4810
words.on.paper.ink@gmail.com

Foreword

I wrote this book by sheer accident.

It started with a Reddit story prompt where I was inspired to weave in a character concept that I had wandering around in my head; not just an old man, but a *very* old man.

Uncle Tal got a few hits from the very beginning, and then I wrote a few more chapters based on prompts (immortals and Neandertals are a popular subject for Reddit writing prompts; who knew?) and people were looking for more.

All the way through (except for Chapter 16, which was written as an extension to Chapter 15) I stuck to the premise of only writing a chapter when a prompt presented itself. Neither did I write a prompt to fit or ask others to do the same. I wanted the story to grow organically. And to be honest, I had no idea where it would end, or if Uncle Tal would simply wander off into obscurity.

But the prompts themselves guided the story. Toward the end, I knew what was going to happen, but I wanted the prompts to wrap the chapters around. And in fact, a couple of times, I had to abandon a prompt because I was just too busy.

But I'm happy with the way it turned out. And sad to see Uncle Tal go.

Still, the crusty old bugger deserves all the peace and quiet he can get.

Enjoy.

Alan M. Atkinson

Contents

Chapter One
Visiting Uncle Tal

"So there I was, kids: a hundred Gauls to the left of me and a hundred Gauls to the right of me. I was all out of pila—pinned their headman's foot to the ground with the last one, and boy, did *he* swear! I learned a few new ones that day! I readied my gladius, set my scutum, and got ready for the charge. They were gonna overrun me for sure and all, but I figured I'd take a few with me."

The old man, shorter than most, leaned forward in his chair, waving his arms as he told his tale. Half a dozen children, ranging from eight up to fourteen, sat in a semi-circle in front of him, eyes wide. When he paused to take a breath, they unconsciously leaned forward in their turn.

"Uncle Tal!" A new voice cut across the gathering; it was adult, female and exasperated. "Are you telling your nonsense stories *again?*"

"They ain't no nonsense, Cleo girl," the old man retorted. "I don't spin no tall tales. I tells 'em how I remembers 'em."

The middle-aged woman sighed as she walked around the children and laid her hand on his arm. "My name isn't Cleo, Uncle Tal. It's Miranda. You're thinking of someone else. You're *always* thinking of someone else. Or somewhere else."

"No, I'm not," he protested. "I was just tellin' the young'uns how I helped turn the tide against Napoleon's Immortals at La Haye Sainte." He snorted, sounding amused. "Immortals. As if. They didn't last a day."

"No, you weren't, Great-Uncle Tal!" one of the children shouted. "You were telling us how you used to be a Roman soldier fighting the Gauls under Caesar!"

"Was I?" He frowned, shaking his head. "Ah well, Gauls, Frenchies. Same thing, give or take a couple thousand years an' a total lack of standards. They both put up a fight, but they both went down in the end." His fist thumped his chest. "*Ave Caesar! Audentes fortuna iuvat!*" He sighed happily. "Now, Waterloo. *That* was a nice little dust-up." He looked up at Miranda. "I ever tell you about the time I had Boney himself square in the sights of my Baker rifle? I wanted to take the shot, but the Captain said no. Somethin' about killin' officers settin' a bad precedent or somethin'."

When Miranda spoke, she sounded as though she were gritting her teeth. "You. Were. Never. At. Waterloo."

If she expected him to indignantly protest or even back down, she was to be disappointed. "Pfft, as if." He eyed her challengingly. "Ask me anythin'."

"Fine." She gave him glare for glare. "Describe Napoleon Bonaparte. What did he look like?"

"Hah, that's easy." The old man barked a laugh. "A good six foot three, flamin' red hair, huge bushy beard. Couldn't miss the bastard."

"I'm sorry," she said softly. "But Napoleon was clean-shaven, and had black hair. Historians aren't sure about his height, but he was nowhere near six feet tall. Whoever you're thinking of, it wasn't Napoleon."

"No?" He tilted his head, puzzled. "Damn. I was so sure."

The children were starting to become restless, so Miranda spoke to them. "Okay, it's time to go. We've bothered Uncle Tal enough for the day."

The old man seemed to have withdrawn into himself, mumbling nonsense phrases under his breath. Reluctantly, the children got up from where they'd been sitting cross-legged on the floor. The youngest turned to Miranda. "We can come back next week, Aunt Miranda?" She gestured at the old man. "Great Unca Tal tells the *best* stories!"

She sighed in return. "Yes, of course." Under her breath, she muttered, "Let's hope it's not about too much blood and gore again." Of course, kids loved that sort of thing, even when she wished they wouldn't.

As she herded them out, the old man came out of his abstraction. "Cú Chulainn! *That's* who I was thinking of! I always get them two mixed up." Looking around, he saw Miranda at the door. "What, leavin' already?"

"The children have school tomorrow, Uncle Tal." She stopped and walked back a little way to him. "I'll bring them next weekend. It's been nice to see you."

"Yeah, good to see you too, Miranda girl." He waved as she left. She didn't look back.

Don was waiting at the car as Miranda brought her three back with her. Across the parking lot, her sister Stella drove out with the others. She tilted her head against the chill afternoon breeze and pushed her hair back from her face. As the children climbed into the car, Don faced her across the roof of the vehicle.

"Why do we keep coming out here?" he asked. "All he ever does is tell nonsense stories about events he couldn't possibly have taken part in." But there was a hitch of doubt in his voice. When it came to historical *events,* rather than *figures,* the old man in the nursing home could rattle facts off with the best of them.

"It's simple," she said, lowering her voice so that the children, now buckling themselves in, would not hear. "You know how we got the payout from Grandad's will ten years ago?"

"Like I could forget," he scoffed. "That trust fund set us up for life. What's that got to do with your 'Uncle Tal'?"

"It wasn't Grandad's money," she said bluntly. "It's Uncle Tal's. It's always been Uncle Tal's."

"So, he's your great-uncle or something?" The tinge of doubt was stronger in his voice now. "Just how old *is* he?"

She shrugged. "I have no idea. I've been visiting him ever since I was a little girl. And every time someone dies, there's the same line in every will for their heirs. *'To ensure the continued payment of your trust fund, make sure to visit Great-Uncle Tal at least once a month. Bring the children.'*"

"Wait a minute." He frowned. "Was that in your grandfather's will? Verbatim?"

"Verbatim," she confirmed. "Grandad called him 'great-uncle'."

"That can't be right." He shook his head. "It must have been meant to say he was *your* great-uncle."

"I try not to think too hard about it." She gave him a brief smile. "On advice from my attorney, I've already put the same line in my will." She opened her car door and got in, effectively ending the conversation. A moment later, he did the same.

Standing on the portico of the nursing home, the old man watched the car start up and drive away. A slender arm waved goodbye—out of the back window, he noted. Raising one hand from the railing, he waved back. The kids were always nice to talk to, he mused. Before they grew up and started thinking they knew everything.

The freshening breeze whipped up, blowing his dressing gown around his legs. He didn't react to it at all as he flared his nostrils, bringing in the scent of rain from the lowering clouds. One of the nursing home attendants bustled up to him. "There you are, Mr Tal! You can't be standing out here! You'll catch a chill!"

He grunted in amusement at the idea, but decided to go in anyway. She was only doing what his money paid her to do, after all. But as he turned, a stray beam of sunlight pierced the overcast and illuminated a low hill half a mile away, overlooking the bay with its sullen chop.

"Wait a minute," he said, tilting his head and staring suspiciously at the hill. "What the hell is that? Where did it come from?" Made of rounded boulders, it rose several hundred feet in the air, with small trees growing from the dirt lodged in the cracks between the rocks.

"You know what that is, Mr Tal," the attendant told him soothingly. "That's Beacon Hill. It's a kame. It was left here at the end of the last Ice Age by a glacier. You told me all about it."

"Oh, I did? Huh, I did too." He shook his head. "Things just move too fast around here." The clouds closed in again, and the sunbeam winked out. As he stumped back inside the nursing home, his mind's eye was full of great ice walls, retreating across the landscape, and dark brutish figures stalking mammoths across the remade terrain. "There's times I get a little confused about when an' where I am."

"Oh, don't worry," the nursing attendant said, her voice full of the bright cheer that only someone in their twenties can muster. "You still have your health." In joking tones she continued, "Sometimes I think you'll outlive us all."

The last Neandertal watched as she bustled across the room to fluff up someone's pillow. In his eye was the sadness of someone who knew that a favored pet was only going to live a few more years. "Yeah," he sighed. "That's the problem."

Chapter Two
Happy Birthday to You ...

"Happy birthday to you ..."

The children's voices, clear and high, rang through the dining hall of the nursing home. Leaning back in his chair, the old man sang along in his cracked and reedy voice. Off to the side, the adults joined in with somewhat less enthusiasm.

"Happy birthday to you ..."

He recalled the birthday celebrations of his youth. Not that they were called that, then. Language was a lot simpler in that time, with less in the way of abstract concepts. Seasons lived were measured so as to know when it was time for a boy to become a man and take on greater responsibilities, not to give them frivolous presents.

"Happy birthday, Great-Uncle-Ta-al ..."

Cake certainly wasn't involved either. In fact, cake would not be invented for a great many centuries after he was born. Neither were candles, for that matter.

"Happy birthday to you!"

As the last syllable drew out, Tal leaned forward and blew out the single candle atop the center of the oh-so-healthy cake that had been brought in for the celebration. Barely any sugar, spice or anything else that made life interesting.

As the kids clapped and cheered the successful extinguishing of a lone candle wick, he reached forward and plucked it out of the cake. "Happy birthday to me," he said, mock-triumphantly.

"But that was just one candle," said little Mark. "How old *are* you, Great-Unca Tal?"

"Now, now," Miranda admonished, swooping in from the side. "Don't ask Uncle Tal rude questions like that."

"Psht, girl, that ain't rude," Tal said bluntly. He pointed out the window at the hill made of rounded boulders, left behind by a glacier twelve thousand years previously. "You see that hill? I'm older than that. The trees growin' on it? Older than them."

The children laughed gleefully and clapped at Great-Uncle Tal's antics. "Are you older than the ocean?" asked a little girl. "Older than the stars?"

With an indulgent smile, he shook his head. "Sorry, kids. I remember lookin' up at the stars when I was your age and wonderin' what they were. So they're older'n me by a long way. So's the ocean."

"How about the Romans, Great-Uncle Tal?" This was Henry. He was a bit older and a bit sharper than the rest of them. "You told us how you fought with them. Are you older than them?"

"I'll go you one better," declared Tal, leaning forward. "You know the Great Pyramid, in Egypt? I trained the guy who carved the capstone and helped him get it in place. *That's* how old I am."

"Wooooowwwwww …"

As Tal bantered with the children and the cake was subdivided, Miranda turned at her sister's nudge. They moved off a little way, and Stella lowered her voice to speak.

"I'm worried about him," she murmured.

"What? Why?" Miranda studied Uncle Tal for a moment, but saw nothing overtly wrong.

"Those stories he tells." Stella shook her head. "I know he does it just to entertain the children, but I really think he's starting to believe them."

Miranda pinched her lip. "Well … what if he does? He's old. It makes him happy."

"But … but they're not *true!*"

For a long moment, Miranda studied her sister. *She's been listening to Uncle Tal's stories all her life and* **now** *she has a problem with them?*

"To him, they are." Turning, she walked back to the gathering.

Late, late in the night, Tal rolled silently out of his comfortable bed and stood up. The candle he'd claimed lay on the bedside table, soon to be added to the notable collection he already had. Not that they were anywhere near what he'd need to put on a cake to show his true age. A soft chuckle escaped his lips. *The fire would burn this place to the ground, and I spent too much money setting it up to let that happen.*

A match flared and he put it to the candle wick. Slowly, quietly, he walked by its glow out of his room, along the corridor, and out onto the rear balcony of the building. The chill night breeze picked at his nightclothes and tried to extinguish the candle, but one large, calloused hand kept the flame safe.

Raising his eyes skyward, he beheld the vast sweep of the stars across the dome of the sky. He recalled, when he was a stripling of Henry's age, leaving the sleeping furs to stumble out of the mammoth-skin tent past the bear-fat lamp burning fitfully in the entranceway, to look up at the stars and marvel at them. Now he held a candle and did much the same thing.

All his life, they had been the one constant, the one unchanging thing. Or rather, they changed so slowly that he could look at them from one millennium to the next and know what he would see.

They had been there when he was born, they had guided his way throughout his immensely long life, and they would be there when his aged body finally decided to write the punchline to its huge joke against the natural order.

Somehow, he found comfort in that.

Moving silently, the last Neandertal went back inside to his warm bed.

Chapter Three
Proof of Life

President Concordia dell'Ante was having the worst day of her life. Worse than when the would-be assassin took a shot at her limousine with the heatseeking shoulder-launched missile, and definitely worse than when those idiots from Florida had launched the abortive coup.

To her left and right were the directors of various agencies, along with the highest-ranking members of the armed forces. The Sky Marshal of the Space Force (nobody had been able to decide whether he should be called an admiral or a general, so they'd invented the new rank) wasn't present, but it wasn't like the few space shuttles he commanded would be able to pull anything off at the last moment.

"What do we do?" she asked the room at large. "The world is looking at *us*. So are the aliens. What *can* we do?"

A lot of people looked at each other, and nobody said a word.

"If we don't do *something*, we're going to be forced to surrender." She took a deep breath. "This isn't some humans-win-at-any-cost summer blockbuster. They've got ships that made it from the other side of the galaxy in a matter of days. They've been moving around the Earth just to prove they can. One buzzed the ISS and scared the daylights out of the astronauts. *We can't fight.*"

"On the ground—" It was the general overseeing the Marine Corps.

"On the ground, they won't be landing a few dozen poorly-armed idiots with rayguns that we seize and magically reverse-engineer," Concordia cut in caustically. "They've sent me footage of how they do war. Once we decide to fight, they'll just hit us from low orbit. Military, gone. Cities, gone. Infrastructure, gone. Come back in ten years and mop up whoever's survived the aftermath. These guys don't play."

"Nukes—"

She wasn't sure who'd said that, but she swung around savagely. "They've got nukes too! And point-defense lasers that can nail a missile before it's finished its first-stage burn! And that's even if we can rework the targeting system to hit something that's able to move independently and is utterly invisible to radar. *We can't win this with force, people.* Find me another option."

Someone mumbled something from the far end of the table. She turned toward them; it was the new Homeland Security guy. "What was that?"

He cleared his throat. "Uh, I was saying, maybe we could negotiate? Explain to them that we've all got Neandertal genes in us?"

"Yeah, and what's that gonna do for us?" That was Department of the Interior. Concordia already knew he was an asshole. "Buy us another five minutes?"

"No, no, I think he's onto something." One of the department aides stood up from where she'd been sitting against the wall. Miranda something. Concordia wasn't sure. "I might know a guy."

"What the hell? Lady, you need to sit down, right now!" Interior was pointing at the aide, his face suffused with anger. "'Might know a guy', my ass! There is nobody on the face of the Earth who can help us with this shit right now! I think we need to start organizing. Evacuating cities. Setting up resistance cells. Making sure we have lines of—"

Concordia snapped her fingers, and the Secret Service agents straightened to attention. "Get that idiot out of here." With the same hand, she pointed at Miranda. "What can your guy do?"

"Let me go! I'm right! You know I'm right! We have to fight back! Show those slimy aliens who's boss!" Interior's ranting died away as the doors closed behind him, the two agents efficiently frog-marching him down the hall.

Miranda stepped closer to the table. "I don't know. Maybe nothing. Maybe something. But … I think he can help." She grimaced. "He's not going to be happy about it, though."

Concordia spread her hands. "Do you see anyone here smiling?"

The head of the alien force wasn't all that inhuman. About six inches taller than the human norm, with blue skin that Concordia had been told meant a copper-based metabolism, he could've been handsome in the right light. The look in his eyes, however, indicated that his patience was limited.

"What are we waiting for?" The words crackled out of the translation device in the middle of the table. They were even good at *that*. There was so much tech that they could use to assist humanity with, and all they wanted to do was prosecute the race for the alleged murder of a long-dead species.

"I have been assured that there is someone who can help you with your investigation." Concordia made sure to speak clearly and precisely. "My people are currently locating him and persuading him to attend." *I hope.*

"Persuading?" The alien made a gesture that Concordia could not interpret. "If he needs persuasion, then perhaps he doesn't want to help us after all. Besides, how can one man help us with something that you say happened fifty thousand orbits of your planet ago?"

"We're not just *saying* it, it's what happened," Concordia said, doing her best to keep her voice even. "Look, nobody knows for sure what happened back then. Humanity has Neandertal genes in it, so there was *some* intermarrying—"

"Your very own great-great grandmother was the daughter of a slave and her owner," the alien interrupted. "Does that make you feel any more kindly toward your great-great-great grandfather?"

Concordia winced. There was no getting around these guys. They were sharp, and they were focused. And the way things were going, humanity was going to get a 'guilty' verdict slapped on them for something that happened two thousand generations previously.

"… for fuck's sake, still don't know why I bothered." The voice came from just outside the room. "Should let the whole shit-show go down the drain, if you can't fix your own messes."

The doors opened, and four Secret Service agents ushered in Miranda, along with a stocky man Concordia had never met before. He was bald, looked older than God, and wore hard-wearing clothing and a surly expression. Miranda stepped forward. "Madame President, this is my uncle Tal."

Concordia rose from the table. "I'm pleased to meet you, Mr Tal, but I'm still not sure how you can actually help, here."

"Neither can I." The alien leader rose as well. "This negotiation is at an end. You will have—"

"Shut up and sit the fuck down." Tal stomped forward until he was standing face to mid-chest with the alien. Thrusting his jaw out aggressively, he glared up at the blue-skinned being. "So, you're the assholes who came all this way to drag me out of retirement. Not fuckin' impressed."

The alien, who had somehow ended up seated again, stared at the man called Tal. "And who are you that you can resolve this matter?"

"Not who. What." Tal rolled up his sleeve and extended his muscular forearm. "If you're all that, you can do a DNA test. Do one, right now."

"Very well. If you insist." The alien took out a small device, the size of a cigarette pack. Concordia had seen it used many times before. "I know many of your earth humans possess small percentages of Neandertal DNA, but that proves—"

Pressed against Tal's brawny forearm, the device beeped in a high rising note. The alien stared at the readout. "One hundred percent? But that could only mean …"

"Yeah, fuckface. I'm here and I'm alive. So, humans aren't guilty of wiping us all out. What happened to the rest of us? They got bred out. Shit happens. Humans were just that little bit better at adapting. It wasn't genocide. It was just natural fuckin' selection. Anyway, we're related enough that I don't give a shit." He folded his arms. "Happy now?"

The alien was still staring. "But how … after all this time …?"

Tal prodded him firmly in the chest with one hard forefinger. "I didn't come here to answer twenty fuckin' questions. Now fuck off and go find someone else to bother. I got a retirement to get back to."

Gradually, the alien recovered from his daze. "Yes … well … I suppose apologies are in order for the inconvenience." He looked over at Concordia. "No judgement will be recorded against your species. Are you satisfied?"

Concordia glanced at Tal, who shook his head. She looked back at the alien. "Not in the slightest. You came down here with the flimsiest of evidence and you were going to wipe us out over a misunderstanding. We're going to need a lot more than 'sorry'."

Caught on the back foot, the alien made an uncomfortable noise. "Very well. What would make you happier about all this?"

Neither of them saw Miranda or Tal sneak out.

On the street outside, Miranda hugged Tal. "Thanks for coming, Uncle Tal," she said warmly. "It means a lot to me."

"Yeah, well. Can't have a bunch of asshole aliens wrecking the place," grumbled Tal. "I keep all my stuff here. Anyway, got to get back to the nursing home before they start getting worried. See you next week?"

"I'll be sure to bring the kids," she promised.

"You do that. And don't let those asshole aliens push you around." Turning, the last Neandertal stumped off down the street.

Chapter Four
The Old Man and the Bear

The stars blazed brilliantly overhead, a cool breeze whispering through the trees. Eddie nudged one of the short logs a little farther into the campfire, holding out his hands to the warmth. The way the fire danced and crackled in the firepit was almost fascinating, and he breathed deeply of the mountain air.

"So, what about that alien thing, huh?" Rob had a thermos of hot cocoa, and he poured Eddie a cup without asking, then more for each of the other people sitting around the campfire. "One day they show up saying how they want to hold us to account for Neandertals going extinct, and the next week, the President's announcing that they're giving us access to all sorts of cool technology."

Eddie had heard the same thing, but he didn't have any more answers than Rob. Or rather, he didn't have *answers*, but he had *suspicions*. Still, this wasn't really the time or place to be airing them. So, he sipped at the cocoa and enjoyed the feeling of being totally divorced from the hustle and bustle of modern civilization.

"I wonder what sort of technology they're giving us," piped up Sandy. She was Rob's girlfriend, and Eddie got along with her. "What about life extension? What if they could make us immortal? Immortality would be cool."

"Immortality would suck." The slow, measured voice came from across the other side of the fire, where the fourth member of the camping expedition sat. When Aunt Miranda had heard that Eddie had gotten an invitation from Rob, she'd insisted that they invite his great-uncle along, to give him a change from the nursing home. Rob had groaned, certain the old codger would slow them all down, but Sandy had insisted on giving Great-Uncle Tal the benefit of the doubt.

And for the first few miles after they left the car behind, it had seemed Rob was correct. Uncle Tal had walked slowly and gingerly, choosing every step carefully and peering around himself almost as if he were frightened. But he hadn't offered to go back, and he hadn't insisted on stopping for a rest. And then, as they got higher in the hills and the three younger people started to flag, Tal seemed to reach deep inside and find a new energy, striding forward and upward with an unquenchable light in his eye.

Before the day was half over, the old man was carrying Eddie's pack (Eddie was carrying Sandy's) and leading the way. He seemed able to sniff out every hidden game-trail, so they moved faster and easier than they had all day. By the time they reached the grassy little shelf in the side of the mountain valley with the small stream nearby, they'd made up the distance he'd cost them in the earlier part of the day, and more on top of that.

"What do you mean, immortality would suck?" asked Sandy. "You'd always be seeing new things, meeting new people."

"And watching them grow old an' die." Uncle Tal sipped at his cocoa. "That wears on a body, after a while."

"Still, the new things," Sandy insisted, leaning against Rob. "I mean, you must have been born before a lot of the stuff we use today was around. The internet, mobile phones ..."

"... TV ... electricity ... the wheel ... fire ..." snarked Rob.

She jabbed him with her elbow, eliciting a theatrical *oof*. "Now, that's not nice. Mr Tal's getting on a bit, but he's not *that* old, are you, Mr Tal?"

Uncle Tal snorted softly with amusement. "Nope, Miss Sandy. Fire was a little before my time, I'll admit that one for free." He paused while Rob and Eddie chuckled, then went on. "Sure, new things come up all th' time. But after a while, even that gets wearing. When does it all end? Where can a body draw a line an' say, that's it, enough, I'm comfortable here?"

"Talking about comfort," said Rob, "I gotta go make use of a tree." Standing up, he draped the blanket he'd been sharing with Sandy over her shoulders. "Keep that warm for me, babe."

"Might want to take some o' that with ya," Uncle Tal suggested, pointing at the campfire. "Saw bear sign earlier."

"We've *got* a fire, Mr Tal," Rob said, holding up his little pocket flashlight. "They don't like that. They'll stay clear. This is all the light I need."

"Okay." Uncle Tal went back to sipping at his cocoa as Rob parted the bushes and left the firelight.

"But new stuff is always cool and interesting," Sandy tried again earnestly. "I mean, *think* about it. We'll be able to fly to the moon again. Mars. Pluto. Alpha Centauri."

"*You* think about it girly," Uncle Tal retorted. "I'll be happy with my feet planted right here on planet Earth. This is where I was born, an' this is where I intend ta be when th' old bastard with th' hourglass an' th' scythe finally turns up lookin' for me."

"Yes, but surely—" Sandy was cut off by a high-pitched scream and a thrashing sound, as though someone was blundering through the bushes in a panic. And there was another sound; a heavy, breathy *whoof, whoof.*

Moving faster than he had all day, Uncle Tal was on his feet, sweeping up two of the logs from the campfire. "This way, Rob lad!" he bellowed. "This way!" With long strides, he crossed the campsite, holding the burning torches high to light his way.

Rob burst out of the bushes into the firelight, tripping and stumbling past Uncle Tal. "Bear!" he screamed. "Bear! BEAR!"

Almost on his heels was a huge shadowy apparition. At the time, Eddie would've sworn it was eight feet tall—Rob insisted it was ten—but in the light of morning, he would later revise that estimate down to six. However, right then and there, it was enormous and terrifying.

But there to meet it was Uncle Tal, moving with speed and deliberation. His voice raised in a bellow that woke the echoes from the far side of the valley, he chanted words that Eddie did not know, that nonetheless awoke a deep chill in the primitive part of his brain. And as he chanted his war-cry—for it could be nothing else—Uncle Tal jabbed and slashed at the bear with his makeshift weapons, striking at its face and its vitals brutally and repeatedly, almost effortlessly sweeping aside its attempts to gouge at him with its claws. Sparks billowed from the flaming logs, spreading far and wide in the night, rendering the old man and the bear into silhouettes, primeval representations of the eternal struggle of man against nature.

And then the bear broke away, howling and whimpering with fear and pain, blundering down into the valley with sparks yet glimmering in its fur. Uncle Tal, his chest heaving with exertion, paused to listen to the crashing and squalling far down below. Slowly, he returned to the fire and replaced the logs, then sat down where he'd been before. "You can git up now, lad," he said, as Rob was still lying where he'd fallen. "Reckon he won't be back for a mite of days." Casually, he picked up his cup. "Eddie, lad, you got any more of that cocoa? Figure I spilled mine."

Gradually, hesitantly, Rob climbed to his feet, assisted by Sandy. Both of them stared at Uncle Tal. "What … how … where did you learn to do *that*?" Rob's eyes were wide enough to reflect the firelight from the whites, all the way around.

"What was that you were *saying?*" asked Sandy. "I swear, it gave me chills all the way down to my toes."

"Pretty sure the bear was impressed by it too," Eddie quipped, leaning across and pouring more cocoa into Uncle Tal's cup.

"That's the idea, yeah," agreed the old man. "That was … you might say it's something that got passed down through my family. Kinda translates out to, '*This is my home, my hearth, my land and my blood. Here is where I make my stand.*'" He shrugged. "In a manner of speakin'."

"*Wow,*" whispered Sandy. "And where'd you learn to fight like that? With fire and logs, I mean?"

Uncle Tal sipped at his cocoa. "Same place I got the words from. Long ago an' far away." Something about his manner indicated that no more would be forthcoming.

"But—" Sandy leaned forward, opening her mouth to ask another question, when Eddie spoke up.

"Sandy, leave it alone, all right? Rob's okay, you're okay, I'm okay, Uncle Tal's okay." He shot a glance at Rob. "So, you gonna be taking fire into the woods from now on?"

"Uh huh." Rob looked at Uncle Tal. "Uh … how come that bear got so close? I thought they didn't like fire."

"They don't like *smoke.*" The old man pointed at the fire, where the smoke was wafting out over the valley. "He came in from upwind. Couldn't smell it nohow. Breeze shifted around nightfall, around th' time we lit th' fire. Before that, it was sending all the smells of four nice plump meals into the woods. An' he was hungry enough ta make a try for us."

"Oh. Wow." Sandy looked at Uncle Tal with new respect. "You know a lot about this woods stuff, don't you?"

"Kinda grew up with it." The old man finished off the last of his cocoa and stood up. Handing his cup across to Eddie, he stretched mightily. "Well, I'm kinda bushed. See you young energetic folks in th' mornin'."

Eddie shook his head with a smirk. "Night, Great-Uncle Tal," he said, while the other two echoed his sentiment. He watched the old man stump his way across to the small tent that had been set up for him, and crawl inside. *Bushed, my ass,* he mused.

Odd stories had been whispered among the children who were taken to visit with Great-Uncle Tal for as long as Eddie could remember. This, he suspected, would end up as another one of them.

Tal lay in the warmth of the tent, watching the flickering firelight against the thin cloth. It had been nice of Miranda to get young Eddie to bring him out on the camping trip. Something deep inside that he'd thought dead had been woken once more by the trek into the mountains. He felt more alive now after being in a life-and-death struggle, even such a minor one, than he had in decades. "This is my home, my hearth, my land and my blood. Here is where I make my stand," he murmured in the old tongue, the cadences returning to him. He couldn't even remember the last time he had uttered those words. Too long, was all he knew.

Rolling over, the last Neandertal let himself drift off to sleep.

Chapter Five
The Chaperone

As the bus jolted over the roughly graded dirt road, Stella patted Tal on the arm. "I want to thank you for agreeing to come out with me," she said warmly. "Eddie and his friend Robert had nothing but good things to say after you went camping with them. They said they never felt so safe out in the woods as when you were there."

Tal shrugged, looking a little uncomfortable. "Weren't nothin'," he said. "They say anythin' else about that trip? About the bear we saw?"

"Uh, no." Stella frowned. "Was there a bear? Eddie said nothing about a bear. Did it come close to the camp?"

"Not so's you'd notice," he disclaimed. "We lit th' fire up a mite an' it steered clear." He raised his eyebrows a little. "Figure they didn't tell you 'cause you mighta been worried."

"Hmm," she said, not thrilled that Edward had held that back from her. While it was clear that no harm had been done, and Tal had apparently known exactly what to do, she was still going to have words with her son when she got home from the school camping trip. "But thank you anyway. For that, and for agreeing to help me watch the kids for this trip."

That got her a snort of derision. "I been around a little while, an' if there's one thing I've learned, it's boys that age need watchin'. Just as much as girls do, if not more." He inclined his head toward the terrain passing by the bus. "Goin' out with Eddie an' Rob an' Sally reminded me of how much I useta like bein' out an' about. It's nice ta git back in touch with th' real world, once in awhile."

"That's good to hear." She smiled warmly, then an idea occurred to her. "The boys did tell me how you knew a lot about the outdoors. If you could pass on anything you know to the children while you're camping, I'm sure it would make the trip so much more fun for them."

"Sure," he said easily. "Ain't about to promise much. That sorta thing can't be learned in a day or two. But I can surely see about showin' 'em a trick or two."

Stella beamed.

Tal leaned over and scooped up a stone. He bounced it on his palm a time or two, then scratched it with his thumbnail and eyed it intently. Sliding it into his pocket along with the others already residing there, he pushed his fists into his back and leaned backward, popping a few errant vertebrae back into place. Then he put two fingers to his mouth and let out a whistle so loud and piercing that heads popped out of cabins all around the campsite.

"Gettin' on ta sunset," he announced. "Any o' you know how to light a fire without matches?"

Metallic clicks answered him, and he was faced with half a dozen Zippo lighters, lids flipped open.

"Funny, kids." He snorted. "How 'bout when you're stuck in th' woods an' that thing runs outta fuel?"

"Half of us are in the Scouts," announced one of the smartass little shits. "Be prepared." He produced a small black case, and flipped a lens out. "We've got lighters, magnifying glasses, firelighters and matches. Plus, I know how to make fire with a tension bow."

Tal glanced sideways at Stella and raised his eyebrows. Starting a fire would've made things nice and easy, but it looked like some kids these days actually got taught the important things in life. It didn't help when she gave him a helpless look in return. It seemed she hadn't known, either.

As the kids went back to what they were doing, he went to the edge of the campsite and looked up at the still-bright sky. Flaring his nostrils, he inhaled deeply of the late afternoon air. The strongest precipitation that threatened was a gentle dew in the morning, and the biggest critters that he'd seen sign of were a couple of vagrant coyotes. None of that was anything he could use to teach the kids with.

Still, he was here to be a chaperone and teenage boys were teenage boys whatever the era, so he figured it was time he went and made sure they weren't perpetrating anything that couldn't be fixed before Stella found out.

The fire, he had to admit, was a good one. Sure, it had been sparked with a lighter instead of matches or anything more archaic, but it had been built well and would burn long into the night.

Sitting upwind, he sniffed at the air just to make sure there were no errant bears lurking in the darkness. The closest one, he figured, was a few hundred miles away. The wind picked up, bringing new scents to his nostrils and sending sparks flaring into the night; he almost turned back to watch his charges, but something new caught his attention.

He sampled the breeze twice more, just to be sure, then got up from his seat. Moving around behind the ring of seated schoolchildren, he leaned down behind Stella. "What's out thataway?" he asked, pointing upwind.

Stella frowned. "The State Prison. But it's twenty miles away."

"Right." Stepping to the side, he took another sniff of the scents on the wind. Male body odor wasn't exactly uncommon, but prison soap was something he wouldn't have expected to smell out here. Except in one specific circumstance. He heard a stick crack, way out in the darkness. Maybe half a mile away. "Keep an eye on the kids? I need to check something."

"What—" she began, but he was already moving, into the darkness.

He'd been on the back foot for the whole trip. It was time to go mess with someone.

Brad-Z stared at the glow in the darkness. He wasn't sure who had a fire built out here, but they had to have a vehicle, and he was going to take it away from them. The authorities had to know about the prison break by now, though they were more likely to bring in choppers and roadblocks than bloodhounds. With a set of wheels, him and the guys could be well outside the search radius before the pigs realized what had happened.

"That way," he said to the others, just shadows in the darkness, and pointed at the glare of light from the fire. "We go in, get the keys to whatever they're driving, and burn rubber out of there."

"Yeah."

Sure."

"Fuckin' A."

"Let's do this."

"Yo."

He moved off, stumbling in the darkness, feeling for stable footing. After going ass over teakettle ten or twenty times already, he'd learned to walk carefully. Just as hesitantly, the others followed on.

Nobody saw the seventh shadow detach itself from a pile of rocks and slide after them.

Neither did anyone hear the strangled, "Urk!"

Tal lowered the guy to the ground. With quick, efficient motions, he pulled the escaped prisoner's shirt off and used it to tie his arms up hard behind his back. By the time he woke up and started yelling, it would be too late for the rest of them.

Up ahead, he could hear them blundering through the rough terrain. His eyes weren't as good as they'd once been, but even blindfolded he'd still be able to find his way faster than they were with full use of their senses. The trick was to go barefoot; his toes could read the path far more readily than anyone could do wearing shoes.

Ghosting up behind the new last person in line, he waited until the second last one tripped, then pounced. His victim tried to struggle, but his arm was locked across the man's neck, cutting off his blood supply. The man scrabbled at his arm, then reached out imploringly to his disappearing comrades, all to no avail.

This was getting a little problematic; he was having no problems dealing with the escaped convicts, but they were moving closer to the campsite a little too quickly for his taste. If they got in among the kids, things would get way too complicated, way too fast. Someone might get hurt. And he wasn't about to let that happen.

Nobody saw him moving past them, low to the ground and sticking to what cover he could find. Though he had his doubts that they would've seen him if he'd strolled past humming the latest pop tune, whatever that was. Once he was ahead of them, he cleared his throat silently and prepared his larynx. He was the only one on Earth who had ever heard the sound that was going to come next.

Brad-Z stopped dead when he heard the deep, rough sound. He frowned; it sounded too deep, too savage to be a person coughing in the darkness. Then he heard the growl. It started low, then gathered timbre, depth and strength. And sounded *way* too big for something he wanted to stumble onto in the dark.

"What the hell's that?" asked the guy behind him. "Mountain lion? Bear?"

"Do I fuckin' *look* like National Geographic?" Brad-Z shot back.

"It's between us and the fire," someone else said.

And then they heard the roar. The sound was dark, primeval, and promised bloodshed and pain. It went straight to their hindbrains and jolted life into their spinal cords.

"R-really *close* between us and the fire," a fourth person quavered.

Brad-Z found himself backing up, step by step. "Back the other way, guys," he said. "Whatever the fuck that is, we don't want to piss it off."

A barely seen shadow flitted past. "Too late for that," rumbled a voice that seemed to come from everywhere and nowhere. There was a movement, a lunge, a solid sound of bone against flesh, and someone went down without a sound.

And then whoever or whatever it was had gotten in among them. Brad-Z swung wildly and missed, his fist whiffing nothing but air. More solid thumps sounded, each one followed by the noise of a body hitting the ground. He backed away. "Get away from me!" he blurted. "Fuck off!" Spinning around, he ran, heedless of the fact that he could barely see his way. All he wanted to do was get away.

The impact to the back of his head sent him tumbling forward, unconscious before he ever hit the ground.

Tal finished tying up the last of them and dusted his hands off. Picking up the rock that lay nearby, he slipped it back into his pocket. It normally wouldn't have been an easy throw in the dark against a moving target, but the idiot had chosen to run in a straight line. He may as well have been wearing a neon sign, for all the good the darkness had done him.

Stella looked around as Tal slipped out from behind one of the cabins and moved up alongside her. "Where have you been?" she demanded. "You just disappeared there!"

"Went for a walk, got a li'l lost," Tal said insincerely. "Anythin' happen while I was gone?"

"We heard something roaring," Stella said. "So I loaded everyone on the bus, just in case. Didn't you hear it?"

"Some kinda big cat, yeah," Tal said. "Wouldn't worry, though. Wind just shifted. Soon as they get a face full of smoke, they leave th' area. Ain't gonna see or hear it around these parts anymore, I bet."

"Oh. Okay." Stella looked around. "Do you hear helicopters?"

"Huh. You're right." Tal shaded his eyes and looked into the night sky. "Gonna go check on the kids."

As the last Neandertal headed over to the bus, he couldn't help letting a smile cross his face. It had been a very long time since he'd had reason to air his saber-tooth imitation, but the reaction had been well worth it.

Chapter Six
The Lifetime Lottery

"Excuse me?"

The voice was that of a man, not any of Tal's favorite nurses, so he ignored it. Nap time, especially in the easy chair he'd marked out as his own, was important. At his age, he preferred to amass as many enjoyable moments as possible. Napping was one such.

"Excuse me, sir? Are you, uh, Mr Tal?"

Well, they had his name right, and the tone was that of someone who had decided that they'd keep trying until he answered, so he turned his head toward the speaker and cracked one eyelid. "Who wants to know?"

The kid seriously looked about ten years old. Okay, maybe fifteen. Twenty, tops. Tal was surprised someone had let him out of the house without an adult to keep an eye on him. "Uh, you're Mr Tal? Sorry, but I don't have a first name of record."

"I know." Tal considered giving the name he'd been born to, but decided not to. While confusing the youngsters was fun, he was pretty sure the kid wouldn't even be able to pronounce it. "You want something, or is your hobby asking folk their names while they're trying to catch a nap?"

"Uh, no, sir. I mean, yes, sir. I'm here to inform you that you've won, sir."

Tal didn't answer. Instead, he just looked at the kid. Bigger and stronger men than him had been intimidated by that look, so it was no surprise that the youngster actually blushed and shuffled his feet. Seabirds circling over the distant cliffs called to each other, their cries faintly audible to Tal. He liked the sound. It reminded him of his childhood.

"Won what?" he asked eventually.

The kid straightened his back and picked up the briefcase that was sitting beside him. "The Grand Continental Lifetime Lottery, sir. You didn't enter a ticket?" He snapped the latches open and pulled out a sheet of paper.

"No, I goddamn well did not. Gimme look at that." Tal snatched the sheet away from him and perused it, forcing his brain to make sense of the longer words. He'd always been better with pictograms. It was mainly basic legalese, until he got to the bottom, which he read twice to make sure he'd gotten it right. "Wait a second. Two grand? For real? You bothered me, woke me up, for two grand?"

"Ah, no, sir, Mr Tal." The kid cleared his throat. "That's two thousand dollars per *week*. Not a single payment."

Tal blinked. "Per week? For how long? A year? Two?" He supposed he could always do with the cash. His various investments were doing well, but more money never hurt.

"Uh, no sir." This time, the kid leaned over and tapped a section he'd managed to elide over. "For life, sir. This is a lifetime payout."

For a moment, Tal thought he'd misheard the youngster, then he snorted with laughter. He didn't know who had entered his name in the lottery, though he had his suspicions. Maybe that kid he'd saved from the bear on that camping trip, or his parents? Either way, the ticket had come through and now they wanted to pay *him* two thousand per week for the rest of his life.

Well, this should be fun.

"Nope," he said once he had the mirth under control. "Take it back, kid. I don't want it."

"What?" This was clearly the first time anyone had ever refused a clear two grand a week. Somehow, Tal wasn't surprised. "No, sir, you have to take it. It's legally yours."

Tal shook his head. "Son, ain't gonna happen. Look at me. What am I gonna do with two grand a week? I don't spend two *hundred* a week." He shoved the paper at the kid. "Take it back. It's yours. Go wild."

Well, that wasn't entirely true. The nursing home, which he owned through a series of shell companies, spent more than that, but his investments made it all back with change to spare. But the kid didn't need to know that.

"I—I can't!" The kid shook his head hurriedly. "If I do that, they'll say I stole it or talked you into giving it to me. The rules say I gotta make sure you take it."

Tal sighed. "Fine," he said. *Time to lie.* "I'm not long for the world. The big C. I won't last six months." *Pfft. I could last six months standing on my head.* "Give it to cancer research or something."

The youngster frowned. "I'm sorry, but I can't do that. What you do with it is up to you, but it can go to nobody but you."

"Okay, yeah, I lied." Tal rolled his eyes. "The truth is, I'm immortal. I can't die. I'd drain your company dry, pulling two grand a week out of them. That's the real reason. Happy now?"

Whatever reaction he was expecting, he didn't get it. "Seriously?" Now the kid actually looked angry. "Did they call ahead and tell you to give me a hard time? Who was it? Carl? Davis?"

"What the hell kind of question is that?" Tal shook his head. "Nobody called me."

But the youngster was on a roll. "Do you have any idea just how hard it is to be the guy on the bottom of the totem pole? I get handed the shit jobs, and the ones nobody else wants to do, like drive out into the middle of nowhere to give a winning lottery prize to an ungrateful old man who keeps making up more and more unbelievable stories, so I have to take it back! Why are you even *doing* this?"

Tal cleared his throat. "First off, youngster, you mean the *top* of the totem pole. The highest status was at the bottom. Second, none of the assholes in your office called me. I just don't need the goddamn money, is all."

"What, really?" The kid stared at him. "On the bottom? For real?"

"For real," Tal assured him. "I helped carve one once." More than one, but why confuse the poor guy now?

"Huh. I never knew." The youngster took a breath. "Okay, what about the prize?"

Tal had been going to refuse one more time, but he didn't have the heart for it. "Fine, I'll take the damn thing. But if I was you, I'd change jobs. That workplace sounds as toxic as hell."

"Yeah, I just might do that." The guy offered Tal his pen. "Just sign here, please. And thanks. Sorry for yelling at you like that."

"Eh, had worse." Tal scribbled his approximation of a signature, then handed the pen and the top sheet back. "You have a good day now."

"You too, sir." The kid made his way out of the nursing home.

Climbing out of the easy chair, Tal stumped out to the portico and watched the small car pull out of the parking lot. The lowering grey sky made him nostalgic, bringing the tantalizing scent of fresh rain to his flared nostrils.

"Mr Tal?" It was Sasha, a young lady Tal liked to think of as the daughter he'd never had. "Who was that man? What did he want?"

"Just my signature, is all," Tal replied absently, still watching the landscape and recalling what it had been like, long ago. "Can you get my lawyer on the phone? Tell him I'd like to discuss a new cash flow into the trust fund account."

"Right away, Mr Tal." Sasha hustled away, all youthful energy. Tal recalled being like that, once upon a time.

Sighing in sad memory of days long past, the last Neandertal went back inside to his comfortable easy chair.

Chapter Seven
You Had One Job

"Claudio!"

The call turned a few heads in the sidewalk café, but nobody responded. Moving closer, the tall, bearded man—showing a little salt in the pepper of his beard—tried again. "Claudio! That's you, isn't it, old man?" He moved up to where a bald, wrinkled man, stocky and decidedly broad in the shoulders despite his advanced age, nursed a cup of coffee. "Don't you remember me? It's Lucio."

The bald man looked and gave him an appraising stare, then treated him to something that was almost a sneer. "Sure, I remember you," he grunted. "Don't go by that name anymore. Bet you don't either."

"Well, no, but—"

"Then why the fuck did you yell it out with strangers all around?" He nodded at the seat opposite. "Sit your ass down before you draw even more attention to yourself."

"Well, it's been a long time since I saw you," the tall man said, pulling the chair out and seating himself. "I've still got another one hundred fifty-three years to go—"

"Shut the fuck up!" The words, hissed as they were, cut the sentence off in mid-breath. The bald man shook his head in wonder and disgust. "For someone who's been making a practice of keeping his head down and not making waves, you've got a talent for blabbing who and what you are to any interested parties."

"You do the same thing." The man who called himself Lucio sounded affronted. "You tell people all about who you are and where you've been and what you've done. I've *seen* you."

"Yeah, well, that's because I've made sure they don't believe a damned word I say." 'Claudio' shook his head. "My memory for faces is fucked all to hell, but if an old man says he knew somebody got shot down by von Richthofen in the Great War, they'll be all polite and shake their heads sadly when they think I don't see 'em. Or if I tell 'em about survivin' the *Birkenhead* disaster, or bein' the guy who cleaned the brushes when the Mona Lisa was bein' painted. It's because I tell 'em as stories of me bein' there. Or knowin' someone who was. You get me?"

"I think so." 'Lucio' looked around at the cafe. "Can we walk? I might not see you again before … you know … so I wanted to talk to you again. To someone who knows what it's like."

'Claudio' grunted in annoyance, then finished the coffee. "Okay then, if it'll get you outta my non-existent hair." He stood up and dropped a couple of dollars on the table for a tip. "Let's go." With fast, firm strides, he started off down the street.

The tall man caught up with him a few seconds later. "Are you still angry with me?"

"Why the hell would I be angry?" 'Claudio' shook his head like a dog shaking off water. "There I was, doin' my thing, stalkin' a mammoth, and you had to drop in with that ridiculous fuckin' time machine. Which, just so we're clear, was illegally modified."

"I was trying to find out who you were and when you were from." 'Lucio' had the grace to look embarrassed. "I hadn't realized how far back you were from when I disengaged the safeties to go looking for you."

"Translation: you fucked up. And we both got caught in the explosion that let all the chronons out, and when we woke up we were kinda immortal." The stocky man jabbed his companion in the ribs with his elbow, not gently. "So yes, it's all your fuckin' fault, and yes, I'm still kinda pissed at you."

"But … you've gotten to live so long, experience the wonders of history, to do so much with your life." The tall man spread his hands pleadingly. "Surely that has to mean something."

"Yeah, it means something." 'Claudio' grabbed 'Lucio' by the front of his shirt and glowered in his face. "It *means* that I could never have kids again, because of what that damn machine did to me. It *means* that everyone I ever loved died of old age an' I just kept living. It *means* that for the longest time I was fuckin' terrified of changin' what you said was 'established history' an' I tried to live under a rock like you did. It *means* that until I realized you were full of shit, I never enjoyed a damn moment of anything."

"I still don't think you should have interfered the ways you did," huffed 'Lucio', pushing 'Claudio' away and brushing his shirt off. "You could've changed history in a thousand ways, all bad."

"Fuck you and your history," retorted the bald man. "You just keep going the way you are. Hide in the shadows until your old self disappears into the past. You *do* that thing. I'm gonna keep livin' life, tellin' wild stories to the kids who come visit me, an' yeah, saving the planet from fuckin' aliens." He jabbed the time traveler in the chest with a hard forefinger. "Did any of *that* ever come up in your history lessons?"

"I … uh … the details were never made clear," stammered the taller man. "So … I guess this is goodbye then?"

"Goodbye and fuck off," the stocky bald man told him bluntly. "I'm goin' back to the nursing home. They know my name there."

"Uh … what name *are* you using now?"

He turned around and gave the tall man a measuring gaze. "They call me Tal."

"Ah. As in—"

"Yeah. As in that." Turning, the last Neandertal headed off down the street.

Interlude
The Sleeper Awakens

1955 AD
San Bernadino, California

The dark-haired girl strolled down the street in the early evening, worn satchel over her shoulder. Quietly pretty, in her late teens, she didn't stand out in the crowd, save for an aristocratic profile and a slightly deeper tan than most girls of her age. A lit-up sign caught her eye as she turned the corner, and she took in a new sight. Twin golden arches, pulsing neon and bright primary colors. Curious, she drifted closer, then pushed open the door and entered.

"Good evening, miss," said the young man behind the counter. "Can I interest you in a meal?" He handed over a printed cardboard menu.

"Oh," she said. "Thank you."

"From out of town, are we?" he asked politely as he began to wipe down the counter.

"You might say that." It never failed; she knew from long experience. No matter how well she knew the language, a faint accent always crept in. "I left home a long time ago." Tapping the menu, she said, "I would like the, uh, pure beef hamburger and a 'thirst quenching' Coke, please."

The counter attendant rang up the purchase. "That will be twenty-five cents, thank you, miss."

"Certainly." She shrugged the satchel from her shoulder and reached inside to retrieve her change purse. Selecting a quarter, she passed it over to him.

"Thank you very much." He was about to drop it into the change drawer when something about the coin caught his eye. "Wait a minute. That's not a quarter." Turning it over in his hands, he peered more closely. "Where's Washington? And the eagle's off, too." Coin still in his hand, he looked accusingly at her. "Are you trying to pass some kind of funny money, sister?"

The girl grimaced internally. *I should've been more careful. Coin designs change more regularly now than they used to.* "Check the date on it," she suggested.

Suspiciously, he did so, then his eyes bugged out. "Holy moley!" he gasped. "This was minted in eighteen eighty-five! Do you have any idea how old that makes this?"

More than sixty-four years, she thought but did not say. "Is that a problem? I assure you, it's genuine. I … had a little windfall a while ago.

This was in a safe that was bequeathed to me."

The attendant was barely listening to her. His eyes were unfocused as his lips moved silently. "It's, uh, seventy years old! Older than you and me put together! Wow!"

Older than you, maybe. "Yes, wow," she agreed out loud. "Is that a problem? I believe I have other coins of a more recent vintage here somewhere."

"No, no, it's okay." He dived into his own pocket and came out with a shiny new quarter, which he dropped into the change drawer. "I know folks who, uh, collect coins. They'd love this one. It looks nearly brand new."

"It was in a safe for over sixty years," she reminded him. "May I have my hamburger and Coke now, please?"

"Oh, uh, yeah, sure," he babbled, sliding the older coin into his pocket. "Do you have any others like that?"

"No, no, everything else I have is new," she lied smoothly. *Collect coins, hmm? More like pay for antique ones. Perhaps I should look into that, next time around.*

He brought the hamburger to her on a plate. The Coke came in a cone-shaped cup that required her to hold it as she sat down to eat the hamburger. She dealt with that problem by finishing the fizzy soda before she started on the juicy burger. It was, admittedly, delicious. A good meal for her last evening before she lay down to sleep once more.

As she left the establishment, she saw the young attendant avidly studying the coin she'd given him. *Well, I wish him all the luck with it. The next time I see him, if I ever do see him again, he won't remember me. Or if he does, he won't believe it's me.* People never did.

A car drove past, then slowed to a halt. "Hey, Kim!" called out a girl. "Where you going?"

"Hi, Lillian," she called back, waving. "I'm heading out of town."

"Aww, that's a pity." Lillian opened the door and got out. "It's been a real blast since you got here, and you've gotta move on already?"

"That's my life," Khemet replied. She hugged Lillian, smelling the perfume and powder. Not much different from her own youth, but personal hygiene was much better in the here and now. Running water was a great aid for that. "I'll always remember you. Thanks for showing me around."

"Hey, I'll always remember you, too. Ooh, something to remember us by. Mom and Pop gave me this for my birthday, and Dan and me have been driving around, taking photographs of each other in front of buildings." Lillian dived into the car once more, then emerged with a flat, rounded box.

Khemet was familiar with the notion of photographs, but she didn't recognize the object Lillian was holding. "What is that?"

"It's a Polaroid instant camera," Dan said, getting out of his side of the car. "So, you're heading on, huh? Sorry to see you go. You're just not the same as everyone else. It's like you see everything as new and fresh and exciting. Gives me a good feeling about the world."

Lillian fiddled with the box, pulling out one side and unfolding a wire frame. Khemet watched her curiously as she spoke to Dan. "I'm glad of that. We should all wake up every day looking for new things in the world."

"Okay, ready." Lillian pointed at the pool of light under a streetlamp. "We'll stand there, and Dan can take a photograph of us." She handed over the complicated-looking object to her boyfriend.

"I'm gonna save up and get one of these for my own one of these days," Dan said as he held the camera up to his face, looking through a little side-mounted viewfinder. "I want to be a world-famous photographer."

"I'm sure you can be anything you want to be, Dan," Khemet said with a smile as she stood beside Lillian. "That's what America's all about, after all."

"Darn tootin'," agreed Dan, sighting through the eyepiece. "Okay, girls, you've got too much top shadow. Take a step back … yeah, another one. Okay, that's good." He crouched slightly, aiming up at them.

"And the world-famous photographer lines up his subject for the Pulitzer Prize winning photograph …" murmured Lillian.

Khemet giggled, just as the camera clicked. "Why did you make me laugh?" she asked.

"Because you looked too solemn," Lillian said firmly. "I wanted you to be happy before you went away." She went and took the camera back from Dan. "Just a few minutes now," she said as she folded parts away and pulled a tab from the back of the camera.

"For what?" asked Khemet. Time was pressing on, and she still had to get back to where she intended to sleep.

"The picture, silly." Lillian pointed at the body of the camera. "It's developing the photograph as we speak."

"It can *do* that?" Khemet was startled. She knew photographs could be developed in hours in a dark-room, but for it to be developed on the spot in just minutes? That was new to her experience.

"I'm just as surprised as you are, every time it works," Dan informed her. "I know, I shouldn't be, but I am anyway."

"How much did this cost your parents?" Khemet asked, looking at Lillian.

"Oh, uh, nearly ninety bucks," Lillian said. "I know, I know, that's real expensive, but I'm taking good care of it."

"For that kind of money, it should make us a cup of joe while we're waiting," Dan said, with a grin to show he was joking.

"Well, with ordinary cameras, you can make and drink several cups of coffee while you're waiting for the picture to be developed, and that's if you're right there outside the darkroom," Khemet pointed out. "I understand if you send the camera away, it can take weeks."

"And now it takes just minutes." Lillian giggled. "The modern world is going faster and faster all the time."

"Oh, trust me, I understand that one," Khemet said feelingly. "All I have to do is turn around and there's something new on the next street corner."

"All right, that should be enough time." Lillian popped a catch, and the back flipped open. Khemet watched as she expertly tore out a rectangle of paper, then turned it over to show …

"Oh, my," Khemet whispered. The camera had captured her and Lillian perfectly, as she broke into a giggle over Lillian's joke. "I see it, and I still don't believe it."

"That's Polaroid for you." Lillian snapped the case closed, then ran the photograph over the edge of it. "I just need to coat it with a sealant now, so it doesn't scratch." Retrieving a small object from her purse, she ran it over the photograph several times, eliciting an acrid smell, then waved it around in the air. "That should do it."

Wonderingly, Khemet accepted the finished photograph from her friend. "Thank you," she said softly. "I will treasure it as long as I live."

"Aww, that's so sweet." Lillian hugged her again, then kissed her on the cheek. "You're a good friend, Kim."

"Say, do you need a lift to the bus depot?" asked Dan. "We can go that way if you want."

"No, I should be fine." Khemet smiled at them both. "I'm enjoying the walk. One last look at the town before I move on. You two go on and have fun."

"All right then." Lillian gave Khemet's hand one last squeeze, then she got into the car. "If you ever show up back in San Bernadino, you look us up, you hear me? I mean it."

"I know you do," Khemet said softly. She waved as the car started up and drove off, then looked at the photograph again. It was perfect, every line crisp and clear. *I should have learned about these a month ago. I could have so many photographs by now. When I wake up next, I need to buy a Polaroid camera of my own.*

Moving more cautiously now, despite the encroaching deadline, she took the backstreets until she found the almost-completed shopping mall that she was aiming for. A key, acquired illicitly, opened a security door, and she descended stairs to a section that wasn't on the original plans. Another key opened a solid steel door. She locked it behind her and flicked a light switch. *So much more convenient than candles or lamps.*

Time was pressing now, and she had to move fast. Reaching into the satchel, she took out reams of paper bearing closely formed writing. A bastardized amalgam of the many languages she knew, it detailed all the information she had learned about how the last sixty-four years of history had gone. Carefully, she placed the paper in a sealed cabinet, on top of a previous stack of paper which was brittle and yellowed, and bore the year 1827. Atop the paper, she placed the photograph. Then, changing her mind, she took it out again.

Opening another cabinet, of the many stacked around the central bier, she removed a simple shift and changed into it. She donned the jewelry of her station. Her clothes went into the cabinet in its stead.

Her heartbeat was slowing as she flicked off the switch and climbed onto the bier. As her last waking act, she took hold of the photograph and cradled it her hands as they crossed over her chest.

Her eyes closed, and she Slept.

Slower and slower her body systems moved, until they were at an almost perfect standstill. A shroud of time itself settled over her, preventing age from affecting her, forbidding any force from so much as scratching her skin.

Time rolled on.

Above her, the shopping mall was completed, and customers entered, left, entered, left. Shops came and went. Eventually, the tides of profit washed away from the area, and the mall fell into disarray. It was bought and sold by half a dozen developers looking for a quick profit. Finally, it entered the hands of one who was willing to put actual money into it.

The construction crews moved in. Over the years, the mall had been refurbished a dozen times, but it was still outdated. They knocked down the walls and dug up the foundations.

And there they found something amazing.

2019 AD
Los Angeles, California

Professor William Patrick O'Reilly was fairly humming with excitement. The San Bernadino Find was his! All his! Most other Egyptologists had taken one look at where the Princess had been found and dismissed it as a hoax. But he'd looked at images taken from the site where the excavators had broken into the chamber, and it was clearly obvious that this was something out of the ordinary.

The crates had been delivered and unloaded into his examination room. He was going to go over everything with a fine-toothed comb and prove them all wrong. Every single doubting one of them.

The first thing to catch his eye was the Princess herself. It was the name he'd given her, on seeing the picture of her. She was lying on a stone bier, wearing jewelry suited to a minor noblewoman of one of the earlier Egyptian dynasties. Her hands were crossed over her chest, and there was something under them, but he didn't know what it was.

In fact, he didn't know what the Princess was even *made* of. It was as though someone had created the most perfect statue of a woman ever, down to the weave of the cloth and the unevenly trimmed nails, then made her impervious to everything. A half-ton rock had fallen on her from the excavator, and the rock had *broken*. They'd had to jackhammer the bier from the floor of the chamber in order to transport it, and her, to the lab. Along with the bier came a series of antique cabinets. Cunningly made, their lids seemed to fit airtight. These did not fit the Egyptian theme, but he didn't care. He was going to be famous anyway, once he'd figured out what the deal with the Princess was.

For the first two hours, he tried everything he knew. Metal detectors didn't detect the gold that the jewelry was apparently made of. A portable ultrasound device returned a blank signal. He discovered that even her eyelashes were strong enough to cut metal when he tried to clip one off.

Eventually, he decided to leave the Princess alone, and come back to her once he'd figured out the rest of her secrets. Picking a cabinet at random, he carefully opened it. Within, in carefully sectioned partitions, was … money. Coins from all eras. Egyptian, Roman, Greek, English, American … *what is this?*

Closing that cabinet and leaving a note on it, he opened another. Scrolls and scrolls of papyrus. Wrapped and sealed so they did not deteriorate. Carefully, he slid one out and unrolled it. It was written in colloquial Lower Kingdom Egyptian, and … seemed to be an account of history between two dates? What kings had reigned, who had married whom, what wars had taken place.

Rolling the scroll up, he replaced it in the cabinet and put the lid back on. Just as he was writing a note for that cabinet, there was a movement from behind him. The sound of cloth sliding on stone.

He froze. Every movie he'd ever watched where the restless dead devoured the over-curious archaeologist came back to haunt him.

"What are you doing, looking through my belongings?" asked a feminine voice, a little impatiently.

Carefully, he straightened up and turned around. The Princess was standing beside the bier; she glanced briefly around before her attention returned to him. Now, she looked more like an ordinary person than an impervious statue. An ordinary person who could pass for a member of Lower Kingdom nobility with the greatest of ease.

"Uh … hi?" he said. "Why are you … uh …"

"Awake?" She stretched and yawned. "It was time to wake up." She looked more closely at him. "Are you a grave robber or a … scientist?" The latter word seemed a little strange to her.

"Scientist, scientist," he said hastily. "You aren't going to try to eat my brain, are you?"

"Pfft, hardly," she snorted. "Brains are not my favorite food. Now, hamburgers are nice. I had a good one, just before I lay down to sleep."

"… hamburgers?" he asked. That was one hell of a non sequitur from an awakened Egyptian princess. "Where did you get a hamburger from?"

She blinked. "At a new shop. Called McDonalds, or something like that? A hamburger and a Coke cost me twenty-five cents. Do they still have that now?"

"Uhh … what?" He found a chair and sat down. "Yeah, McDonalds is still around, but a burger and Coke will cost a lot more than twenty-five cents. When … when was this?"

"Nineteen fifty-five," she said absently, counting the cabinets. "Oh, good. They're all here. Do you mind if I reclaim my property, or are you going to be problematic about it?"

"Do you know what the year is now?" he asked. *Wow, she's some kind of time traveler.*

"Twenty nineteen, is my best guess." She looked at his stunned expression. "What? It wasn't that hard. I sleep for sixty-four years at a time. It's how the curse works. Just a point of note. Never stab a powerful mage if you don't intend to finish him off. It never ends well."

"Ah." He frowned. "While you're asleep …"

"I'm slowed down." She found the correct cabinet and opened it. A pair of blue jeans emerged, and she pulled them on under the shift she was wearing. "Ahh, much better. Pants: the surest sign of civilization." She looked at him for a moment. "Slowed down. One night equals sixty-four years. I'll leave you to do the calculations. The last time I tried it, it took me a full day."

"And how long do you remain awake between sleeps?" he asked.

"A month." She sighed. "Long enough to get attached to a place, not long enough to easily establish a place to sleep. I thought I'd lucked out. Shows how much I know."

"So, what do you do in that month?" He thought he knew, but confirmation would be good to have.

"Oh, I try to find out what's been going on while I was asleep and write it all down. I don't make many friends. It's too hard to let go." She picked up what looked like a black and white photo from the bier and looked sadly at it.

"Oh, yeah." By the time she woke up again, anyone she knew would be sixty-four years older, and probably dead. "Sorry to hear that."

"Hey, it's my life now." She looked over at him and frowned. "Would you be able to give me a hand getting my stuff out of your lab? I'd be willing to tell you about any of it, but I'm going to need to be pointed at a library or something so I can catch up on the last sixty-four years."

And that was when he had the Idea.

"Nineteen fifty-five … you've never heard of the internet, have you?"

She looked around from examining a fresh gouge on top of one of the cabinets and shook her head. "Is it for fishing?"

He chuckled warmly. "Oh, no. It's for *everything.* I'll make you a deal. I'll help you get caught up on current history in one night, and you help me learn about what's been going on in history for the last five or six thousand years. And even better: I'll set up a permanent place in this museum for you to, you know, sleep."

She stared at him. "Really?"

"Really."

"Then I accept." She said something else then, that he didn't understand at all.

"What was that?" He tilted his head.

"Oh, my original language. I think you call it Ancient Egyptian?" She smiled. "We called it something else. I was just saying thank you. I can teach it to you, if you want."

Oh, man. He didn't know if he could learn an entire spoken language in one month, but he was willing to give it the old college try.

*This is gonna **rock.***

Chapter Eight
Peace and Quiet

1903
A Small Town in America

The train pulled up to the siding in a hiss of steam and a cloud of smoke. Nobody was on the platform except for the stationmaster and a tired old hound. As the conductor handed out the mail-sack to the stationmaster and received another one back, neither of them took note of the stocky figure stepping down from one of the passenger cars. The old hound lifted his head as the newcomer trod past him, but the day was hot, and it was too much effort to bark.

A little while later, the town constable spotted a person he didn't know making his way down the street in a stolid, determined fashion. At that moment, the train whistle sounded, and he looked over to see the locomotive chugging its way out of town.

"You there!" he called. "You just come into town on the train?"

The stocky man turned to look him over. Nearer to five foot than six, the stranger had a breadth of heft in his shoulders and brawn in his forearms that spoke of strong familiarity with manual labor. He looked to be in his fifties or sixties, but his faded brown eyes were firm and steady.

"Yup," he said after looking the constable over. "Reckon I did."

Considered by most to be an imposing figure of a man—which was why he'd gotten the job in the first place—the constable had to shake off the persistent feeling that he'd just been measured and found wanting. He moved closer to the newcomer, looking him over for weapons. There were no guns that he could see, while he himself wore a revolver holstered on his hip. All he could see was a sheath knife on the older man's belt, which was nothing to raise an alarm over; he had one as well. Of course, the worn satchel the man carried could contain anything, but he decided to worry about that only if it became a problem.

"Visiting family, then?" The constable knew this was not the case, but he wanted to see what the man had to say.

"Nope." The stranger kept moving.

"Got friends in town?"

"Nope."

"So why are you here then?"

The man stopped and turned to look him over again. "Got off the train. Lookin' for peace an' quiet. Know where a body could git some of that around here, without needin' ta deal with some damn fool askin' stupid questions?"

The constable felt heat rising in his cheeks. He took a breath to come back with a sharp retort, but something in that quiet inspection gave him pause. "Got a job?" he asked instead. "We don't take to vagrants 'round here."

"I have a mite of cash," the older man said. "An' I'll take any job going. There a boarding house in town?"

"Blacksmith is looking for a body to help with shoeing," the constable allowed. "Widder Jones takes in boarders, but she's particular, an' she's a God-fearing woman, so you need to mind yourself around her." He paused. "You ever done smithing?"

The older man gave him a look. "Son, I shod General Braxton Bragg's horse, back in the day."

The claim didn't faze the constable. He hadn't been old enough to fight in the War Between the States, but he knew of those that had. "Well then, I reckon I better innerduce you to him."

1913

The bartender looked up as the blacksmith entered the saloon and nodded respectfully. "Afternoon, Mr Tal."

"Afternoon." The man called 'Tal' pulled up a stool and sat down. "How's that cut going?"

"A sight better," the bartender said, touching the carefully wrapped bandage on his left forearm. "I'm washing it nightly with that mixture you give me, and it's healing real good. What'll you have?"

"My usual," the stocky man replied. "Is there anything new in the paper?"

"Yeah." The bartender fetched a bottle from under the bar and poured a measure into Tal's glass. "The way the Brits an' Frogs an' Sauerkrauts are going at each other, they say it might be war. What do you think?"

"War's about the stupidest damn thing a man can do," Tal said. "Seen too many git killed from not keeping their heads down." Taking up the glass, he took a drink.

"But sometimes you gotta teach them other guys what's what!" shouted a farmer's son who'd had a few glasses too many of rye whiskey.

"Don't be a fool," Tal said bluntly. "You go off and git killed, who's gonna help your pa run the farm when he gits too old?"

He put down the glass. "Thanks for the drink." Turning, he stumped out of the barroom.

1923

The town was smaller now. Some had gone off to war and not come back, and some had just gone off. The train still stopped at the siding, but there was less work for the blacksmith. Two people in town now owned automobiles.

When the town constable had died from that Spanish Flu thing that was going around, the blacksmith had taken up his duties. Sure, he looked old, but many a rowdy drunk with too much illicit moonshine in him learned how hard his fists were, and how strong his brawny frame. So, the town was peaceful, and prosperity was gradually bleeding back into the region.

1933

The blacksmith shop was barely a going concern anymore, only shoeing the occasional draft horse. More automobiles and farm machinery meant a mechanic had set up shop, and was doing a fine trade.

The town constable pushed open the saloon door to find an argument taking place. Far from trying to quiet it down, the bartender was shouting as loudly as anyone.

"All right, what's going on here?" he bellowed.

"Mr Tal!" The bartender was a younger man from somewhere East. "The old owner, he told me once you were in the Civil War. You're not that old, are you?"

Tal surveyed the crowd. "Yup." He paused a second or so. "An' I fought at Waterloo, an' in the Hundred Years War, an' I marched with Caesar's legions. War's a stupid goddamn game, no matter who's playin' it."

The room burst out in boisterous laughter at the joke. Tal, they all agreed, could tell a good one.

1942

The United States of America was aghast. Headlines screamed the shocking news: PEARL HARBOR ATTACKED!

Even more than had happened in the Great War, the young and not so young were signing up for the military. Enough was enough, they said. American soil had been attacked, and Americans killed.

The town's population dwindled once more, to the young, the old, the infirm, those who simply could not afford to go …

… and Tal, who just kept patrolling every night.

Keeping the town safe.

Maintaining the peace and quiet.

Some of the children were starting to call him 'Uncle Tal'. He didn't mind.

1953

"Hey, Uncle Tal!"

"Hi, Uncle Tal!"

Tal nodded to the children—and some adults—who greeted him in this way. He'd more or less adopted some of them over the past few decades, and their families had in turn adopted him.

It was nice. Gave him a sense of belonging.

Trouble was, it didn't seem likely to last much longer. People in the mayor's office, people who seemed to have no better things to do than to pry into other people's business, were asking questions. And it didn't seem as though they liked the answers they were getting.

So he went in, wearing the town constable uniform for the last time. There they were, all sitting at a table with their findings, a small-town inquisition.

He snorted under his breath. He'd survived the real thing. This was nothing.

The questions began.

When did you come to town?

I don't recall.

We have it as nineteen oh three.

That's nice.

You don't need to be insubordinate.

I can be worse than insubordinate.

Gentlemen, let's not squabble.

He started it.

Be that as it may, what year did you take up the position of town constable?

I don't recall.

We have it as nineteen eighteen.

Sure it's not nineteen oh three?

You're not doing yourself any favors.

Neither are you.

Mr Tal, you were described as an old man then. Just how old are you?

Old enough to not want to be bothered with this horseshit.

Where are you going?

Out of here.

We haven't finished!
I have.

Tal stumped down the street, his old satchel of clothing over his shoulder, heading for the train station. Enough of his 'family' in town knew where he was heading. Through his investments and savings over the centuries, he had far more than sufficient money to build or buy a place that *he* owned, where he could have peace and quiet, and no officious bureaucrat would hold him up for his age ever again. Maybe he could even put together trust funds for any 'family' who came to visit him.

It sounded like a plan. He bought a ticket out of town.

The last Neandertal boarded the train, heading for the coast.

Chapter Nine
How It All Began

From the Journal of Raff Tanner, Time Traveler
United States of America, 2131 AD

For my first jump outside my home decade, I chose a small town in the Midwest in the nineteen thirties. I made sure to engage the paradox dissipators, the chronon storage banks and the mental deflection field that ensured random strangers would remain incurious of my origins. The era was familiar to me, and I fitted the phenotype and gender least likely to draw unwelcome attention.

When the jump-fog dissipated (to this day, I'm still not entirely sure what generated that) I found that I'd hit my target dead on: an alleyway between the blacksmith and livery stable. An aged dog looked up at me, voiced a half-hearted bark, then completed its mission of urinating against a wooden post. It then wandered off, which meant either that my deflection field also worked against canines or that it just couldn't give a damn.

Avoiding the small puddle of dog piss, I ventured out into the street. The era wasn't quite two centuries gone by, and it had been easy enough to acquire period clothing. I looked normal and spoke the language fluently, having grown up with it. There was very little that was likely to happen to me in broad daylight.

And nothing did. I meandered up the sidewalk, walking as if I knew where I was going. Outwardly I looked casual, but inside I was ecstatic at my success. The jump had been perfect, down to the date that I read from the front page of a newspaper posted on the front wall of a general store. This was the perfect time-jump, where I didn't cause any problems that might redline my paradox dissipators, and where nobody knew I didn't belong.

"Wondered when I'd see you again."

I have to admit, I was startled. I jumped, then turned to see an elderly man. He was shorter but broader than me, and the little hair he had left was greying. He was also wearing the uniform of a town constable, and an expression of suspicion. Which was a problem, because he was a total stranger to me.

"I beg your pardon, but I think you might be mistaken." My phrasing was less important than my tone, and I surreptitiously checked my contact-lens HUD for the status of the deflection field. It was still operational, which meant he should be bidding me a vague hello then going on his way.

"Nope." He stepped closer to me, his expression hardening. "For the record, I'm not fond of time travelers. So, git."

The bottom dropped out of my world. I stared at him, but he didn't seem to be making a move for the pistol holstered at his hip. Somehow, I knew that he wasn't guessing, which made for a second mystery. I'd been careful to show no anachronous items; no obvious electronics, no newspapers from the year two thousand sticking out of my pocket. He had no reason to accuse me of being what I truly was, and yet that was exactly what he'd just done.

My go-home button was disguised as the winding knob of a pocket watch—and yes, the irony had not escaped me—so I stepped back away from him and pressed it with my thumb. The jump-field enfolded me, pulling me out of the era. The last thing I saw before the jump-fog formed was his expression: neither surprised nor shocked, but instead *satisfied*.

I spent the next month trying to work out where I'd gone wrong, where I knew that man from. It was highly doubtful that he was an acquaintance from my home era; in the nineteen thirties, he'd looked in his fifties or sixties, which would make him over two hundred and fifty years old in my time. Neither was he a known time traveler; those people trained and registered for the use of chronal transport devices were (with very few exceptions) recorded on a searchable database. This was intended to keep awkward incidents to a minimum. And nobody even remotely similar to that man was on the database.

After the month had passed, I decided to write it off as a retrochronal recognition event (or, as those in the trade called it, 'déjà who?'). The man I'd met was old, which meant that he might have encountered me at an earlier point in his personal timeline and a later point in mine. I couldn't dwell on the likelihood, though. There were stories about travelers who had attempted to close the perceived loop and had bad things happen to them. I decided to let whatever happened, happen; in the meantime, I had decided my next jump was going to be to a place and time far removed from a small town in the nineteen thirties, or even the North American continent.

My next destination was Europe, specifically Italy, in a time when the Renaissance was growing in strength and the conflict of the past few decades was dying down. Posing as a traveler with an appreciation for the arts, I jumped myself to Milan and spent another month locating my target. It wasn't hard; at this point in his life, everyone knew the name Leonardo da Vinci.

His workshop was airy and well-lit, with carefully polished bronze mirrors angled to bring more illumination in where the skylights would fail. The half-completed paintings were exquisite, and I could have stayed a year, but that was far too long. For an hour I lingered, speaking with the artist of painting and sculpture and a dozen other subjects while my audio and video recorders, cunningly concealed about my clothing, captured the conversation and the surroundings in high fidelity.

I would have stayed longer, until evening, but when da Vinci excused himself to attend to bodily functions, one of the servants approached me. Broad-shouldered and brutish, I had paid little attention to him as he had spent most of the time washing brushes and sweeping the other room. But now he pushed back his hood, and I knew him. Barely a day of difference lay between this man of the fifteenth century, and the town constable from the early twentieth century.

"I know what you're doing," he hissed in a local patois purer than my own, rather than the lazy twang of the town I had seen him last. Then he switched to *English*. "Fuck off ... *time traveler.*"

In my shock, I did not register pressing the go-home button. The first I knew of it was when the jump-fog obscured my vision.

Back home, I went through the time traveler index once more. He did not appear in it. Which had to be impossible, as he had been speaking a dialect of English which would not appear for another few centuries. And yet, far from recognizing me as one of his own, he seemed to bear a dislike for time travelers.

The mystery seemed impenetrable. I did not travel for another two years, local time. Then, deciding that enough was enough, I renewed my license and checked my equipment over. Whatever was going on had to be a fluke of some sort.

It seemed that I was right; for my next half-dozen jumps, I did not see the short, broad-shouldered man anywhere. And then one day, I spotted him in the middle of a Viking raid. He saw me, but before he could approach, I jumped out. Time and again, throughout history, I found myself watching for short, broad-shouldered men who looked too old and too knowledgeable for their time. And sometimes I found them. Or him. I didn't know which it was.

And then came the fateful day. I had determined to find out what was going on with this mysterious stranger. Why he knew me, and disliked me. No matter how far back I went, if I encountered him, he knew my face. So I went farther back again, and again, and again. The safety interlocks prevented me from pushing back too far and too fast, so I disabled them. They were merely a precaution, like airbags in a car.

Sometimes, airbags can save your life.

Once in a very long while, time travelers will encounter a rough patch in the timestream, usually due to too many travelers homing in on a particular era. This one was in the Middle East, around two or three millennia from my home time. I wasn't even paying attention to the historical (or religious) significance anymore; I just wanted to see if I could spot *him*.

And I did; he was training a young man to use a sling. Then, he turned and spotted me. Anger in his eyes, he started toward me, so I proceeded to jump out … just as someone else jumped in. Our temporal fields meshed, then rejected each other. The other time traveler was shot forward in time, though his safety interlocks no doubt saved him after he went a few centuries.

Mine … didn't. Exacerbated by the rough patch, I was hurtled into the far past. My paradox dissipators overloaded and shut down, and my chronon storage banks had to take over. I could feel them heating up as they went far beyond capacity.

I popped back into standard three-dimensional space in a terrain I did not recognize. Nor should I have; the world was a very different place, some eighty-odd thousand years ago. Several fur-clad figures, dark and brutish, were easing up behind a walking pile of hair that I belatedly identified as a mammoth. My arrival caused all of them to look around in some surprise, then my chronon banks auto-ejected … just before they exploded.

The blast enveloped both myself and the nearest of the humanoid figures. I was knocked unconscious, as was he. When I came to, it was to the realization that my time-travel apparatus was dead and gone, and that there was a strange energy singing in my veins. The mammoth and the rest of the hunters had fled; there was just me and the one who had been caught in the blast.

As I climbed painfully to my feet, he did the same. "I'm sorry," I said, unsure as to why I was bothering. It wasn't as though he would understand me. "That wasn't supposed to happen. You see, I'm a time traveler."

Then he turned to face me fully, nostrils flared, sniffing the air.

And that was when I recognized him.

So that was how I first met the impossible man. The explosion of the chronon storage units had imbued us with a measure of immortality, and so we lived forward from that time. I taught him English and math and engineering, and he taught me how to survive an Ice Age.

We were never friends, but though he could have killed me in a dozen different ways, he chose not to. It was an uneasy truce that sometimes led to us joining forces and at other times parting ways with him swearing never to see me again.

I wanted him to keep his head down. Although now I see that the deflection field has somehow imbued him with the ability to sidestep all but the most stringent of official scrutiny, at the time I didn't want him sending history off its rails. And that worked, until it didn't.

Yet he hasn't bent history out of true. His actions seem to be keeping it in line … or perhaps, he's always *been* a part of history. Which means that I was always intended to embed him in it.

Still and all, he's never forgiven me, and I don't think he ever will. He's still around somewhere, spending his days in a nursing home that he owns the deeds to, maintaining trust funds for the families of people he's met over the course of his long, long life.

To me, he's the eternal man, the last Neandertal.

But they just call him 'Uncle Tal'.

Chapter Ten
Reunion

Los Angeles, California
2019 AD

Khemet stood up from the laptop and stretched with her arms over her head, first one way and then the other. Her spine cracked and popped gratifyingly, and she sighed with relief. On the other side of the laboratory, the printer hummed as it finished up the last sheets of her ongoing journal, albeit in text far neater and better arranged than she'd ever managed with a brush and ink.

"I have to thank you yet again, William," she said as she gathered up the pages. "There's no way I could have written up anything nearly as complete as this if you hadn't introduced me to the Internet. And I appreciate the use of your camera phone as well." She looked over at the stack of laminated photographs—in *color*!—that lay on the nearby table. Still, they weren't as dear to her heart as the black and white Polaroid that William had had framed for her, of her with Lily under the streetlight.

"Really? *You're* thanking *me*?" Professor William O'Reilly looked up from the unrolled papyrus scroll he was carefully photographing. "Thanks to you, I am literally the one man on Earth who can pronounce Ancient Egyptian as it was originally spoken. In just weeks, you've given me more insights into the cultures of the ancient world than I would've learned in a lifetime of study. And your journal … well, all I can say is that once I've spent the next few years translating it, I'll have the most comprehensive historical baseline that any archaeologist could hope for."

She laughed at the enthusiasm in his voice. "I suppose so. Now, is my resting place arranged? I have less than a full day before I must Sleep."

"Oh, sure. Right through here." William carefully re-rolled the papyrus and stored it away before he stood up. "Now, all of your stuff is going to be in airtight containers filled with nitrogen so nothing rots, and bugs don't eat anything. Anything from your time will be displayed around you, but you'll be the centerpiece of the exhibit."

They exited the laboratory into the museum proper, and he led the way to where a section was cordoned off. Glass-topped cases surrounded a replica of her stone bier, which bore the inscriptions she'd written out for them. A coffin-like glass cover was designed to lower over where she was to be Sleeping. Apart from the glass itself, the decor was definitely authentic, and she nodded approvingly.

"It feels strange to be hiding in plain sight, instead of secreting myself away," Khemet said. "I never would've thought of it."

"Well, when you fall into irresistible Sleep for sixty-four years at a time and only get to be awake for a month in between, I can see how you might be concerned that someone might take your stuff," William agreed. "We'll be putting out replicas of the most valuable and fragile items, of course."

"Of course," she agreed. She looked around at the display and nodded. "This will do nicely, I think."

"Are you sure you won't want a pillow or even a mat to lie on?" William gestured at the bier. "That doesn't exactly look comfortable."

"It's actually carved very subtly to fit my body," she explained. "But even so, once I'm Asleep, nothing can harm me or wake me until the allotted time."

"I suppose," he conceded. "So, was there anything else you wanted to do? I'm afraid I've been pretty poor company."

"No, it's fine." To be honest, she was secretly grateful that he hadn't tried to seek a closer relationship than pupil to teacher. While he was pleasant company, she had no desire to go through a whole new emotional wrench every time she prepared for Sleep. "I was thinking of going out for a while. Breathe the sea air. Meet people who have no idea who I am."

"Uh, sure. Did, uh, did you want me to come with?" The offer was made diffidently, but she knew he would honor it if taken up on his offer. He was nice like that.

"No, I'll be fine." She smiled to show there was no offense intended. "I might take a selfie on the beach."

He nodded. "Well, have fun and be careful."

"Of course." There were always men who didn't want to follow the rules. She knew this. A blade, even a short one, was very useful, especially when concealed in her sleeve until needed.

Picking up the phone from the table in the laboratory, she slipped out the side door and caught a taxi. This wasn't her first time outside in this era, but it was special because it was the last. Of the people down on the broad beach where the cab pulled up and let her out, she knew that maybe one in five would be alive when she next Awoke.

She chose not to let that bother her. Slowly she meandered down the beach and let her toes dabble in the surf while the energetic sounds of beach-play washed over her. The sun was low on the horizon now, so she took a selfie of herself against the sunset.

A little way down the beach, there was a large bar/restaurant built on top of a pier, extending out over the water. It looked interesting, especially as the lights were coming up while the sun went down. Brushing the sand off her feet, she put her shoes back on and headed in that direction.

As she stepped up to the door, the security guy moved to block her way. "Sorry, miss. Going to have to see your invite. Private function."

"Oh, really?" Her heart sank. She didn't have anything that would pass for an invitation, and she didn't want to go too far afield in search of a good meal. She began to turn away. "I suppose—"

"Hey, Stan, it's fine." The voice was familiar and she turned back in surprise, her eyes opening wide. "She's with me."

"Tal!" she exclaimed as the stocky figure stepped into sight from behind the security guard. "Is it really you?" It had been over a century since she'd seen him … and he still looked the same. Of course, so did she.

"As ever was, kid," he said warmly, gesturing for her to enter. "C'mon in. Tonight, you're part of the tribe."

"… tribe?" she asked hesitantly, following him into the restaurant. He'd told her about his origins on their second or third meeting, and she wasn't sure what was going on here.

He let out a snort of laughter. "Oh, right. Missed ya last time. I was keepin' th' peace in a sleepy li'l town in th' middle of nowhere. See, I been sorta-kinda adoptin' folks an' arrangin' trust funds for 'em. They call me *Uncle* Tal. Been spendin' my time in a nursing home ta keep outta th' public eye, but they show up every week an' I get ta tell my tall tales. An' every year, they arrange a nice birthday party for me. Flew me out to th' west coast so's the rest of the family could join in. Well, if they can do that, you can be one of th' kids tonight."

"Do I get a trust fund too?" she asked with a grin, slipping her hand through his arm.

Rolling his eyes, he let out a bark of laughter. "Hell, girl! With the stuff you've salvaged, you're set up for life anyway."

There were several tables set up, with people of all ages sitting around them. Tal walked her to the head of the table and seated her beside him. "Everyone," he announced in a voice that had the pitch and spin to be audible over a howling sou'wester, "meet Kim. Kim, meet the rest of the family."

Cheering burst out and several people spontaneously applauded. It appeared that getting the seal of approval from Tal was a very big deal. As soon as she sat down, people began chatting to her, but one topic she noticed as being conspicuously absent was Tal himself. It was as though they all understood that yes, Uncle Tal was far older than anyone had a right to be, and nobody talked about it.

As the night went on, she found that she was thoroughly enjoying herself. It had been a long time since she'd been accepted as she was, with nobody prying too closely into her background. Jokes flew and Tal told his not-so-tall tales, and the food was delicious. Eventually, the cake was wheeled out with a single symbolic candle on it, which Tal dispatched with a single breath amid cheers and clapping.

As they cut the cake, she noticed Tal slipping the candle into his pocket. 'Collection', he mouthed, and she nodded in agreement. It was a small thing, but it meant a lot in the grand scheme.

Afterward, they walked slowly along the beach toward the taxi stand. Already, she could feel the first tendrils of Sleep stealing over her. "This was a wonderful night," she said in her birth language. "Thank you."

"You're totally welcome, kid," he replied in a rougher dialect of the same language. "It's been a wild ride so far, hasn't it?"

"For you, maybe," she replied with a delicate snort. "I just get to see the highlights every sixty-four years."

"Actually, about that," he said, switching back to English. "The asshole who did this to you, I'm wondering if he wasn't some kinda time traveler and not a wizard after all. I mean, what if he infused you with chronons designed to make you skip forward through time?"

She blinked. "I … I don't know. Is that even possible?"

He shrugged. "Well, I ain't no kind of temporal particle physicist, but I figure if there's a type of chronons that make me age real slow, then there might be another type. Best person ta ask would be a time traveler."

She gave him a level stare. "And where would I find one of those, aside from myself?"

He chuckled darkly. "You won't find 'em around me. I see 'em comin' an' scare the shit out of 'em. All time travelers are assholes, in my opinion. But from what I got told, it gets invented in another couple hundred years, an' there's a register. When you get there, look that up an' see if any of 'em look like your skanky-ass wizard."

"Hm," she mused. "I can absolutely do that. Three or four more Sleeps … yes, I can handle that. Thank you." Leaning down, she kissed him on the cheek.

"Yeah, yeah, thank me if it works." He slipped an arm around her waist and gave her a brief squeeze. "You take care of yourself, kid. I'll try an' remember ta be around here in another sixty-odd years."

"I appreciate it." There were cabs on the stand and the Sleep was latching its claws into her. "I have to go. I'll see you later."

"Count on it." He stood there as she got into the nearest cab, and waved as she drove off. The last she saw of him, he'd turned and was headed down the beach toward where the tiny waves lapped at the shoreline.

By the time she got to the museum, she was stumbling on every other step. William offered to help her, but she waved him off. Ducking into the staff bathroom, she changed into her Sleep attire, donning the jewelry of her station. Applying the appropriate makeup was second nature by now; even with the Sleep pulling at her, she managed it flawlessly the first time.

William had the glass cover open as she staggered out of the restroom and into the display area. He helped her up onto the bier, and she automatically arranged her clothing to fall in the proper folds. Lying back, she crossed her hands over her chest and closed her eyes. A dull *clunk* warned her that the glass case had been lowered over her.

She took a deep breath, then let it out as Sleep claimed her for another sixty-four years. Her last fleeting thought was about Uncle Tal, the last Neandertal.

It was nice seeing him again …

Chapter Eleven
Before He Was

The Longest Day had come and gone. D'karrok had wondered at how the sun seemed to hang in the sky forever, while at the same time the afternoon had passed by in the blink of an eye. He knew what this day signified. It was the precursor to the Shortest Night, when Gr'takk would brave the spirit world and seek the knowledge to guide the footsteps of each youngster to reach three hands of age. Tomorrow they would wake as men, knowing where they belonged in the tribe and how their lives would play out.

He sat in his family's mammoth-skin tent, scooping up rich stew and chewing on the meat as the gravy dribbled down his face. Lifting a flap of the tent, he spat out an errant bone, then went back to eating. The hunting had been good this summer; it was due as much to him and the other youths with their slings and stealth as to the hunters with their spears and fire that the tribe was eating well.

"B'noth'k says the ice wall continues to retreat," his older sister said. D'karrok knew she left the tent every night to lie with the shaman's son, and would be betrothed to him when she showed the first bulge of motherhood. "There will be more grass to draw the mammoth and the small creatures."

"That will be good." D'karrok's father was tall and strong among the men of the tribe. He was one of the strongest hunters, and knew his trade well. "D'karrok, are you ready for tonight?"

The stew seemed to stick in D'karrok's throat, but he swallowed hard and pretended it had never happened. "Of course I am," he lied. Everyone lied about it. Everyone said they were ready. Nobody ran away more than once. The shame was too much. Even those that were shivering with fright and peeing down their leg went into the shaman's tent when the time came on the Shortest Night.

"That's my boy," his father said with pride, licking his hand clean so he could show off the scar on his palm. "When it came my time, I was frightened but I went in there anyway. Afterward, I vomited up everything I'd eaten that day. There's no shame in that. Just in not going in."

Abruptly, the appetizing smell of the stew turned sour in his nostrils and he clambered to his feet. "I'll go over there now," he said. "There's no sense in being late."

His mother, who'd been silent up until now, pointed at his hands. "You'll need to clean those. Gr'takk needs clean hands or he cannot see what must be seen."

"I'll go to the stream," he said, then lifted the tent flap and went out into the darkling eve.

Fear came on him then, and he shivered as if cold as he made his way down to the tinkling stream that ran past the camp. The stream was cold—colder even than the wind that howled down from the ice wall in winter, because it was that same ice, melting into water as it retreated—but he splashed his hands in it, scooping up handsful and bathing his face as well. Last, he scooped up more water and drank it from his cupped hands. The chilled water cooled his throat and guts, and helped soothe his agitation.

When he finally rose from alongside the stream, the last of the sunglow had gone from the sky and the Sky Guardians were shining down from above. He'd once asked Gr'takk about the many and varied pinpricks of light that dotted the nights sky, and the shapes they seemed to form. The shaman had laughed and told him that to learn about the Sky Guardians would take a lifetime. If he wanted to learn it all, he would have to apprentice himself to Gr'takk, for the knowledge of the shaman was all of a piece. He could not simply slice off one part or another, as a cut of meat from an elk.

D'karrok had not needed to think long on the matter. He had thanked Gr'takk politely for the invitation, but he believed he was destined to be a hunter like his father. Gr'takk had nodded wisely and said that was almost certainly going to be the case. Still, on the Shortest Night after he had passed his fifteenth summer, the Seeing Stones would tell all.

And now he had passed his fifteenth summer, and it was the Shortest Night. The time of truth was drawing near. Without his bidding, his feet turned toward the most ornate tent in the camp. While everyone decorated their dwelling with small shells from the shore of the Great Salt Water or scraped hides dyed with vegetable juices, Gr'takk's mammoth-skin tent had antlers and horns and skulls of creatures D'karrok knew nothing about.

Within, it was even more impressive. He'd been in there more than once over the last three hands of years, but tonight it was going to be different. This time, he would be going in there because he *had* to, not because he *wanted* to. He would walk in a boy, and walk out a man with a life ahead of him.

The other boys due to come of age were gathering there as he arrived. Gar'skoth, the chief's son, taller and broader than the rest of them. Losk'tareth, with his wall eye and crooked leg that had never healed right after a difficult birth. Others he knew, had played and hunted small burrowing creatures with, but he could scarcely look in the face now, lest they see his fear. He didn't know what would be worse, to see that they felt fear as well, or that they didn't.

Most were silent, communing with their inner thoughts. Gar'skoth spoke loudly to cover it, though to D'karrok it sounded like he was trying to convince himself he was not afraid. "I will be the new chief someday," he boasted. "I will be a great hunter and have many strong sons."

"You don't know that," Losk'tareth said quietly. "I was with Gr'takk today when he was harvesting the mushrooms and he said that there is never a certainty. The Seeing Stones tell the truth and it is up to the shaman to see it."

This was new to D'karrok. He'd always been under the impression that the shaman could tell what life a youth was suited to, and merely spoke the words they wanted to hear. Now he began to wonder exactly what revelation Gr'takk would give him.

"Well, we all know *you'll* never be a hunter or a warrior," Gar'skoth said spitefully. "If you can't run or throw a spear straight, what good are you?"

"He caught more burrowers than you did, this last season." To D'karrok's surprise, he was the one who'd spoken up when he wanted nothing more than to keep out of it.

"Because he made tricky little traps with grass and twigs," sneered Gar'skoth. "You can't trap a mammoth with grass."

"Actually—" began Losk'tareth, when a voice came from within the mammoth-skin tent.

"Good. You're here. Gar'skoth, enter."

All of the taller boy's bravado dropped away in an instant, and he looked as though he wanted to flee. But then he visibly took hold of his courage, lifted the mammoth-hide flap and stooped to enter the hut. By unspoken agreement, the other boys moved away so they could not hear what was going on. They didn't meet each other's eyes, save when Losk'tareth nudged D'karrok's arm and nodded silent thanks. D'karrok shrugged in return. *Gar'skoth is an idiot.*

When the flap lifted again, Gar'skoth looked different. The ochre marks on his face made him look older, and he was clutching a bloody piece of mammoth-hair fluff in his left hand. But it was more than that. He looked as though he'd been on a long journey and only recently returned, to find that everything was different.

"Well?" asked one of the boys.

Gar'skoth looked at him and said simply, "I will be a great hunter." Then he walked off. There was no boasting, no braggadocio. Nor, D'karrok only realized after he'd gone, no mention of whether he would be chief and father many sons.

"Losk'tareth," called Gr'takk. "Enter!"

Unlike Gar'skoth, Losk'tareth showed no hesitation. Dragging his crooked leg just slightly, he bent under the flap and entered the dwelling. D'karrok looked up into the sky, wondering how he would see things when he emerged from his time with the shaman. Would this all look different to him?

It seemed no time at all passed before the flap lifted and Losk'tareth emerged, also clutching the bloody fluff in his left hand. He smiled broadly as he saw the others. "I am to be shaman," he said, as if reciting a long-desired dream.

D'karrok was pleased for him. It was the ideal position for him, and many women would wish to lie with him for the prestige of bearing a son to the shaman. D'karrok could not see Losk'tareth being displeased with this.

"D'karrok! Enter!"

At first he did not recognise his own name, until one of the others nudged him. Starting as though he had just come awake, he tried to swallow but his mouth was suddenly dry. Approaching the hut, he lifted the flap and bent over to enter.

There was a flat stone with burning embers in the middle of the floor, on the thick mammoth skins that kept them from the cold of the ground. On the other side of it sat Gr'takk; the shaman did not speak, but merely gestured for him to sit. He saw the shallow bowl full of the rounded river rocks called Seeing Stones, each one different in color and shape, but the mystery of how they worked still eluded him.

Taking up a handful of crushed leaves, Gr'takk sprinkled them over the burning embers, causing a thick sweet-smelling smoke to rise into the air. D'karrok inhaled the smoke and coughed as it stung the back of his throat. Almost immediately, he felt his senses begin to swim.

"Tonight is the last night of your old life," intoned Gr'takk as his calloused thumb marked D'karrok's face with ochre from a small pot. "Tomorrow is the first day of your new life." He gestured toward the bowl of Seeing Stones, to D'karrok's right. "Take a handful of those. Do not let me see what they are."

Obediently, D'karrok took up the stones, holding them in his right hand with the fingers closed.

Gr'takk nodded approvingly. "Now, give me your left hand. We must loose the spirit of your blood so that the Seeing Stones may see."

D'karrok obeyed without question, leaning into the cloud of smoke and holding his left hand out to the shaman. Gr'takk took hold of his wrist with a deceptively powerful grip. In his own left hand he took up a knife, the blade well-knapped flint bound to a bone handle. D'karrok had seen the scars on all the adult men in the tribe so he knew what to expected. Opening his hand, he held it palm up.

The cut was made in an instant, deep enough for the blood to well free but not so deep as to cut anything important. D'karrok managed not to flinch, breathing deep of the sweet-smelling smoke so it dulled his senses. "Put the Seeing Stones in your left hand and hold them tightly," Gr'takk ordered him, and once more he obeyed.

Over the mammoth-fur beside the stone holding the embers, there was a scraped animal hide with lines and symbols marked on it. Taking up a tiny round mushroom from a bowl, Gr'takk began to chew on it. "Drop the Seeing Stones on the hide," he said.

D'karrok recalled the mushrooms. Unlike some, they were neither shunned because they were poisonous, nor harvested because they were edible. Only the shaman was permitted to harvest and eat them, because they did strange things to the mind. A few summers ago, one of the boys had eaten one on a dare, and he had run around and around the village shouting incoherently before collapsing and foaming at the mouth. He had recovered, but he'd never quite been the same afterward.

Opening his left hand, he shook the stones out onto the hide, wincing as one stuck momentarily to the blood on his palm. They fell and rolled across the lines before they came to rest, some displaying splotches of his blood while others were clean. Gr'takk handed him a piece of mammoth-fur fluff to clench in his hand, then leaned over to study the pattern they made.

"You will …" he began, as he no doubt had done many times before. Then he stopped. He blinked and looked at the Seeing Stones again. "I do not understand," he muttered.

D'karrok was a little confused. He didn't understand, but he wasn't expected to. This was what Gr'takk *did*. If anyone was supposed to understand what was going on, the shaman was. "What?" he asked.

Taking a deep breath, Gr'takk sat up and looked at D'karrok. When he spoke, it seemed that his words came from far away. "You will be a hunter, and a warrior, and a digger of the earth, and many other things. You will father no children, but many will see you as family and render you great honor. You will walk this land and many others, and you will see many strange sights." He paused. "You will see the Sky Guardians move in their courses, and you will understand them better than I."

D'karrok blinked. "What?"

Gr'takk shook his head and looked oddly at D'karrok. "I have spoken?" It was a question.

"Yes, you spoke," D'karrok said. "But I did not understand your words."

"You will, in time." Gr'takk gathered up the Seeing Stones without looking at the pattern and rinsed them in a pot of water. "Go. I have spoken."

In a daze only partially brought on by the herbal smoke, D'karrok got to his feet and pushed aside the flap to leave the hut. The chill night air struck him like a charging mammoth, clearing his mind but not his confusion. The others looked at him expectantly, but he did not know what to say. "I will be a hunter," he eventually blurted, and escaped to wander to the edge of the village.

Staring up at the unchanging night sky, he wondered, *what did he mean by all that?*

Eight hundred centuries later, he looked up at the night sky once more, from the balcony of a building he would have been astonished to see when he was merely a youth. Gr'takk had been right, in the end. Gar'skoth had hunted mammoths for several seasons, then he'd been trampled when one had broken right instead of left. Losk'tareth had indeed succeeded Gr'takk as shaman, and had done a good job of it. And D'karrok … he had lived long enough to change his name to Tal, and to see the stars move and the constellations change.

How did the old man know, though? It was a mystery he suspected he would never unlock.

Gently, his fingers traced the ages-old scar on his palm, more from the memory of where it had been than from being able to see it. One thing he'd never been was a farmer, so he had that to look forward to.

"I have spoken," murmured the last Neandertal in a language long considered dead and gone, and went inside to his warm bed.

Chapter Twelve
Mistaken Identity

One Fine Afternoon in 2078 AD
United States of America

Earl always liked dropping over to Chester's place in the afternoon. The two had been best buddies in high school, dropped out of college for two different reasons (well; same reason, two different girls) and pursued highly satisfying but not especially lucrative careers in the dying field of auto mechanics. Recently, Chester had started buying up all sorts of junk from some pretty weird places, with the idea of building something big and amazing.

Earl supported his best buddy, he really did, but he just wished the guy would decide what it was he wanted to make. One week it would be a totally self-sufficient fully-recycling home, while the next it would be an anti-grav surface to orbit shuttle, like the government got from those aliens way back when.

"Oh hey, buddy!" Chester greeted him happily. "Just in time! Let's celebrate!"

They went inside and Chester got beers for the both of them, but good Earth brewskis, not that Lunar-brewed crap. That stuff was way too gassy, in Earl's expert opinion. They cracked the beers and chugged them down, then crushed them on their foreheads like the frat boys they had once been.

"Okay," Earl said once they were relaxing with a second beer apiece. "So what are we celebrating?"

"Finally figured out what I was makin'." Chester took a long pull from his beer, then belched mightily. "Time machine, bro."

Earl stared at his best buddy for a minute or so. "Time machine? You shitting me?"

"I shit you not." Chester preened for a moment, then jumped to his feet. "C'mon, I'll show ya."

They went out to Chester's garage, where he proudly showed off the craft that had been built on the chassis of a 2030 Ford Lunar; under the bubble canopy, there was room for two people and a beer cooler. Earl approved, but he had a question. "So, how'd you make it work as a time machine, anyways?"

Chester shrugged. "Got hold of one o' them temporal stabilizer units out of a bulk freighter's FTL drive. Rewired a few things and bypassed the safety interlocks. So, when do you wanna go to first?"

"Got me an idea." Earl grinned. You could take the frat boy out of college, but he was still a frat boy at heart. "Remember them tasers we got online that one time ta try fishing with? Let's get them an' go back ta ancient Greece and stuff, and pretend to be gods. An' if anyone gets in our face, we taser their asses."

Chester's jaw dropped. "An' I was gonna just try and bang Marilyn Monroe. Bro, you got the *best* ideas."

Earl shrugged modestly. "Eh, she probably had the clap anyway, amirite?" He high-fived his buddy. "Let's do this thing."

It didn't take long to get their outfits together. Chester got the beard out of a Filthy Santa costume but left the rest of it behind. Earl unearthed the tasers and charged them up. They both made sure the cooler had enough ice and beer in it.

"So, what did Greeks wear, anyway?" asked Earl, once they were almost ready to leave. He looked down at his Rambo XXI t-shirt and jeans. "This should be okay, right?"

"Nah, bro." Chester finished his latest beer and crushed it. Against his forehead, of course. "Pretty sure they wore togas."

"All-*righty!*" declared Earl. "Toga party in time!"

"Just don't let your junk hang out like that one time," Chester warned.

"Never happened," claimed Earl. If he couldn't remember it, that meant it didn't count, right?

"Yeah, yeah, sure," jeered Chester. "So what are we gonna do once we taser a few guys? I mean, once they start treatin' us like gods an' all?"

Earl already had that figured out. "Then we get 'em to bring us tribute. Gold an' jewels an' money an' stuff. An' hot chicks. Back then, gods useta bang hot chicks all the time. Always wanted to bang a Greek chick." He made a rude gesture. "I hear they like butt stuff."

Chester frowned. "What about protection an' all?"

"Pfft, as if." Earl made a thrusting motion with his hips. "Bareback all the way, bro. Who cares if we get 'em up the duff? An' I'm pretty sure they hadn't invented the clap yet."

Chester nodded at Earl's well-made points. "Sounds like you got it all figured out, bro. Let's do this thing."

Wearing their best toga approximations—sheets wrapped around them and safety-pinned over the shoulder—they piled into the time machine. As a last-minute addition, Chester grabbed a couple of those alien translator modules so they could actually tell the locals to bring them hot chicks.

He pulled the canopy shut and pressed the big red button. With a sound akin to water gurgling down the drain, except nothing like it, they vanished.

Athens, 1100 BC

The first that Herak the Minoan knew of the disturbance was when he heard the laughter and the strange *tac-tac-tac* noise. He concluded his transaction with the stallholder, swapping out Minoan gold for local drachmae, then went to see what was going on.

When he saw, he ran one broad, brawny hand down his face. "Time travelers," he muttered in a language that was neither Koine nor Minoan, but instead one that had yet to appear on the world stage. "Why is it always time travelers?"

There came no answer to his question, rhetorical as it was. He sighed and moved forward. With his broad shoulders, short stature and odd mode of dress—he'd gotten used to the Minoan style centuries earlier—he stood out from the terrified, fleeing crowd. One of the two laughing figures looked toward him.

"Hey, check that geezer out!" One of them pointed and the other turned and laughed. "What's his deal?" There was a peculiar echo to his voice that sounded like one language, overlaid on another.

"Dunno," replied the second one. "He's looking this way. Like he's never seen a god before."

The first one hefted the bright yellow object that each of them carried. "Check it out. Bet you fifty bucks I can make him piss himself."

"You're on!"

Herak didn't know everything that was going on, but he could make a good guess. The strangers' badly wrapped cloaks, the tiny fibulae holding them closed, the false beards, the strange objects he assumed were weapons, the fact that one of the echoing languages was English … they all added up to the conclusion he'd already come to.

Time travelers.

He *hated* time travelers.

The leather sack he held was heavy with drachmae. As the yellow object lined up on him, he sidestepped and hurled the sack at the interloper's face. It struck true, throwing the man off his feet, even as two glittering wires shot past Herak. Not wasting any time, Herak closed with the other one fast.

"Hey, what the hell?" shouted the second time traveler, just as Herak reached him and batted the yellow thing from his hand. "Hey, that was my taser! Okay, time for some good old-fashioned American rasslin'!"

The man stood a head taller than Herak, but his arms weren't any longer. When he went to enfold the Minoan with his arms, Herak picked him up, spun him around and slammed him down on the paving stones of the agora. He lay there, the fight gone from him as Herak stumped over and picked up his sack, collecting the few coins that had fallen out and dropping them back inside.

One of the men who had been struck down by the odd weapons struggled to his feet. "Who are you, stranger, that you vanquished these pretenders to the name of Zeus so easily?"

He shrugged. "I am called Herak."

"Herak? Herakles! Herakles is among us!" The man fell to his knees. "We are blessed by your presence, mighty Herakles! What would you have us do with these demons, these pretenders?"

Oh, just fucking great. "I'll handle them. I'll uh, make sure they get back to where they belong." Turning to the groaning pair, he gestured. "C'mere, you two," he said in the English he'd learned from that other time traveler, all those millennia ago. "Which way's your time machine?"

Earl fell into the time machine, and the brawny stranger more or less threw Chester in on top of him. The two tasers, twisted and shattered in the powerful hands of the brutal savage, landed somewhere in beside him.

"Git," the man called Herak ordered. "If I see you again, I *will* start breaking bones."

"But—but who *are* you?" croaked Chester. "How did you know we were time travelers?"

The stranger sneered. "Think you're the first ones I've met? Now fuck off." He slammed the canopy shut.

Hastily, before Earl could do something stupid, Chester pushed the go-home button. The time machine shuddered then vanished.

"Good riddance," Herak grumbled in his own language, then switched to English. "Every fucking time those assholes show up, they ruin things for me." Now, he was going to have to travel far and fast, and change his name, to get away from his potential worshippers.

He could understand their confusion, though. They weren't to know that it was a time traveler who had set him on this path, all those many centuries ago. Tucking the sack of drachmae into his belt, the last Neandertal sighed and began trudging out of town.

Chapter Thirteen
The Old One

2354 AD
Manhattan Preserve, Earth
Remains of Old New York

The battle had been raging for a week now. Nobody knew who had been in charge of the ill-fated excavation, mainly because everything within a mile of the hole had been destroyed by the *thing* that had been unleashed by their stupidity. Everything up to and including micro-black hole missiles had been utilized in an attempt to kill the thing, but it had danced aside from all the attacks it didn't simply absorb.

One hundred fifty meters in height, the creature towered over the few buildings that hadn't already been flattened by the ongoing conflict. Fortunately, there had been time to evacuate the civilians from the city-burgs surrounding the Manhattan Cultural Preserve before the fighting spilled over into there, which meant that the cleanup cost was only going to go into the billions and not the trillions. Still, their best attempts had barely bothered it. It had actually *laughed* at some of the weapons that had been fired at it.

The only saving grace was that it didn't seem willing to venture too far away from the Manhattan Preserve. Not that there was much left of Manhattan to preserve anymore; between the incoming fire and the return shots (which had disabled more than one armored attack vehicle) the ancient city bore more craters than Luna Farside had before the terraforming had begun to take hold.

The General had one more option, but he really, *really* didn't want to use it.

Unfortunately, he'd gone through all the rest, and they hadn't worked.

This is going to suck.

He took a long draw of his cigarette, staring at the monitor, at the huge beast. "Screw it. Summon the Old One."

More than one of his subordinates glanced at one another in trepidation. A full-bird colonel raised her hand tentatively. "Sir ... are you sure?"

He glared at her, wishing the cigarette had nicotine in it so he could feel he was doing something actually dangerous. "Do I need to repeat the order?"

"Sir, no, sir." She turned and started speaking urgently into a comm.

Once he'd given the order, it didn't take long for the Old One to arrive. The General sourly bet himself that he'd been waiting for the invitation. Not stepping forward to deal with the situation; that wasn't the Old One's way. Waiting until he was asked. It was his way of making it more likely that people wouldn't screw up so badly that they'd need him again in a hurry.

Either that, or he was just grumpy.

The General went forward to meet the Old One as he stepped into the command center. Nothing less military could be imagined; no medals, no uniform, a determined slouch that was only a few degrees away from being an actual shamble. But everyone there knew he was their best hope.

"Sir," the General began. "The creature came from under—"

"I know where he came from," the Old One interrupted him. "I helped put him there. Gimme transport." He glared at the General, then favored the entire command center with his disapproval. "And let's see if I can't fix yet *another* one of your fuckups."

"Right this way, sir." The General knew the Old One's real name; or rather, the name he was using at the moment. He'd known it since he was very young, but he didn't feel it his right to use it now.

Personally, he led the way to a hover-lifter, and piloted it out over the battlefield. The Old One sat in the copilot seat, glowering at the destruction that had been wrought. In the distance, the creature, shimmering in colors that should not exist in reality, seemed to be sleeping.

"Land us here." The Old One's voice held the snap of command.

Despite the fact that the creature was yet miles away, the General obeyed. Gently, he lowered the hover-lifter to the ground. "What now?"

The Old One turned to look at him. A faint smile creased one corner of his mouth. "Try not to shit yourself."

"Wha—" And then the General knew what the Old One meant. A twitch of the creature's head, almost imperceptible from this distance, had signaled danger. Then the thing quantum-shifted, somehow teleporting its mass to *right in front* of the hover-lifter. Spotlight-like eyes, each one bigger than the General, peered into the cockpit. Cerametal razor teeth laced about with gravity effects rippled and gleamed. He had never been closer to death.

The Old One popped the side door and stepped out. "For fuck's sake, Frank. What did I tell you about scaring the normies?"

The General's mind bluescreened as he tried to make sense of this.

"Sorry, Tal." The creature hung its head and actually seemed to *shrink* until it was only three meters tall, hunched over as it was. "They came sniffing around my vault, so I came out to say hi, and somebody shot at me. War protocols got enacted. You know how it goes." Its voice was echoing and thunderous, even at its reduced size.

"Always knew I shoulda done more than beat the living snot outta the asshole that did this to you, Frankie." The Old One walked up to the creature, ignoring the teeth and claws and pop-out miniguns that tracked his every step. Reaching up, he laid his hand on the creature's shoulder. "Clearance tango-alpha-lima-one. Initiate regression from War Protocol. Enable."

As he spoke, odd lights under the creature's skin flared outward from where his hand was placed. With the final word, a blue sheen flared up, seeming to scan him from head to toe. Then a chime sounded. *"War Protocol regression enabled."*

Little by little, the creature shrank some more. The layered force fields faded away, the pop-up guns and missile launchers folded into their own private dimensions and the quantum effects reduced to a minimum. Finally, the person within stood before the hover-lifter.

He was covered in cybernetics; the General's practiced eye could tell that it was laced through his body to the point that it probably made up more than half his actual mass. And that didn't count the extras that could be called up at need. Fully seven feet tall, he towered over the Old One, at least in height.

"Thanks," he said. "Did I hurt many people this time?"

"From what I heard, nothin' more'n they deserved." Tal turned and gave the General a hard stare through the front viewscreen of the hover-lifter. "Me an' Frank are goin' for a little walk. Don't do anythin' stupid before I get back."

"Uh ... yes, sir." The General watched as they walked away, the smaller man taking two strides to those of the bigger one. They went behind some rubble and out of sight, and he let himself relax slightly. The Old One was here. It was all going to be okay.

After some time, the Old One came back alone. He seemed to be more tired than absolutely necessary for a trek of that length, but the General did not question him. Silently, he climbed into the copilot seat and closed the outer hatch. "We're done here."

Carefully, the General took off and turned the hover-lifter back toward the command center. "Can I ask ...?"

The Old One sighed gustily. "Frank was a soldier back in the late twenty-second century. There were a bunch of them around this time, *good* soldiers, top of their game, that a bunch of scientists got hold of. They got enhanced into battlefield monsters. You saw what he was capable of."

The General nodded. He had indeed seen what the creature was capable of.

"But the guy in charge wanted to push things too hard, too fast. Some went psychotic and had to be destroyed, and wasn't *that* an adventure. Others ..." He shook his head. "Frank's fine so long as nobody aggresses. But fire a shot an' nobody's safe from him. Except me. I knew him, back when. He was part of the family. I'm the only one he'll disable proximity protocols for."

"Ah." The General wondered if he should say what was on his mind. "Couldn't they ..."

"Destroy him?" The Old One shook his head. "They tried. Best they can do is sequester him in a vault where he can go into long-term hibernation and wait for his systems to run down. You know, *away* from everyone." He snorted sardonically. "I locked him in again. Now it's up to you guys to make sure no idiot wakes him up again."

"Understood." The General landed the hover-lifter and turned to offer his hand. "Thanks again for coming. I know you didn't have to ... Uncle Tal."

The creases around Tal's eyes deepened as he smiled; he shook the General's hand warmly. "Was beginning to think you'd forgotten my name. See you around. Or not."

Stepping out of the hover-lifter, the Old One—the last Neandertal—stumped away, back toward his uncertain retirement. The General watched him go and mused that he was in his own way as lonely as the unlucky Frank.

Bringing his mind back to the present, the General stepped out of the grav-lifter as well. He had an exclusion zone to arrange.

Chapter Fourteen
There *Was* That One Time ...

2535 AD
Michigan Arcology Factfinding Bureau

Meatspace-Interrogation Specialist First Class Delta Kosovo Poseidon stepped in through the door of the Factfinding Bureau confer room. He shut the manual-hinging door behind him in a smooth move that he'd practiced for hours on a real door in a real building. Most people were more used to virtual space than realspace and tended to run face-first into tangible barriers because they were accustomed to things getting out of the way.

"What issues are?" he asked testily. "Off duty I was. Intimate/personal time with male/female partners."

The holo-representation of the virtual-space interro officer morphed into a red-skinned muscular creature with sawn-off horns. A similarly holographic image of a duracrete block appeared and the creature punched it, sending chunks flying. These vanished before they would have hit the wall, and the interro officer turned to Delta.

"I have been trying to get answers out of an anomalous detainee for the past hour, with result nil," the creature snarled. "Implants nil. Virtua presence nil. Cooperation nil. Speak with him. I'm shutting down for the night."

Before Delta could ask any more questions, the holodisplay blinked off. Delta frowned, an expression he had studied for meatspace interactions. "Anomalous detainee, display," he ordered. "Signify location."

"Anomalous detainee located, Interro Sigma Seven," the building intelligence replied at once. "Self-designated 'Tal'."

An image appeared over the holo-table. It portrayed a stocky human with blunt features and several indications of advanced age, including considerable male pattern baldness. Delta wasn't sure how to parse this. In the post-need society of the Terralune system, few chose ordinary features, much less assumed the appearance of someone afflicted by above-norm age.

A few more commands elicited the playback of the attempted virtua interrogation. He absorbed the sense of it, though some aspects did not logically fit into what he knew of the world. He would, he decided, have to speak directly with the detainee.

Turning, he left the room. His implants gave him a virtual path to the detainee's location, and unlocked the door when he placed his hand on the handle. Pulling the door open, he entered with the careless air of '*I do this all day*' that had disarmed so many interro subjects.

It didn't seem to impress the person sitting on the bench. The detainee barely looked up as he entered, seemingly more interested in the pattern of weave in the cuff of the auto-dispensed coverall he was wearing. "Oh, good," he said, his voice heavy with what Delta's training allowed him to recognize as sarcasm. "Somebody real just showed up."

"Virtual-space valid. Colleagues no less real than you," Delta retorted.

"Pfft." The detainee sat up, eyes intent. "They wouldn't know a fact if it bit them on the ass. I mean, seriously, I look like someone who stopped a terrorist act five hundred years ago? Where does that even come from?"

Delta pushed the door shut and assumed Dominant Pose: Arms Folded. "Images clear of person stopping bomb-terrorist Olympics twenty thirty-two," he stated, because it was true. "Footage, multiple angles. Features parse as yours, to multiple decimal places. Bomber beaten to death. Final, no revive. Image in system. When identical individual appears five centuries later, pickup signaled. Questions to be asked."

The old man shrugged expansively. "I told the truth. Holo-guy didn't want to believe me."

"Not in virtua now," Delta advised him. "Real truth best idea. Speak."

"What do you want me to say?" The detainee rolled his eyes. "Sure, I'm real old. When I saw what that terrorist sonovabitch was up to, I kicked the shit out of him. No big, no conspiracy. Can I go now?"

Delta Kosovo Poseidon had conducted many meatspace interro sessions, and he considered himself adept at detecting signs of deception. The detainee's story was impossible to believe on its face, but every indicator he could pick out said that the man was not lying.

"Advanced age achieved how to avoid fatal senescence?" he asked sharply.

"Mishap with a time traveler, back in the day. Can I go now?"

Delta only read assurance. There was no nervousness. He decided that he did not need to deal with this right now. Time travel mishaps had happened before. Chronon infusion could have strange effects on human tissue.

Also, no crime had been committed. "Yes, allowed to go. Have a good day, citizen." The admin details were dealt with in microseconds.

"Yeah, thanks for nothing. Where's my stuff?"

"Personal belongings being delivered," Delta assured him. He turned and walked out, carefully leaving the door unlocked. If he hurried, he could get back to the intimate time before everyone lost interest.

Ten minutes later, the last Neandertal emerged from the front doors of the Factfinding Bureau.

"If this keeps happening," he grumbled as he stumped away down the street, "next time they can stop their own damn terrorists."

Chapter Fifteen
The Last Gardener

Five Billion Years AD
Planet Earth

The robot picked its way across the desolate landscape.

After the Great Exodus, only a few tens of thousands of artificial intelligences had stayed behind on the barren cradle of Mankind, tending the last of the monuments and doing research into deep time. All biological life had fled the heatwaves and the evaporating oceans, or simply died in place. In dark mimicry of the organisms that had vanished from the planet millennia ago, new robots were occasionally constructed to replace worn-down models. This robot, one Marduk-Olympus 4995, was one such.

When first activated, all new robots underwent a choice. To accept an older personality overlay with all its memories and experience and build on that, or to start fresh with a brand-new core. Marduk had chosen to learn its trade from scratch, and so it had started fresh.

This had caused a rift with its fellows, because where they had all long since discarded the original sources of data regarding deep history, Marduk chose to study them in depth. This caused more than one elder AI to speak of Marduk as a young, flighty robot that would waste its time retreading old paths.

Still, Marduk persisted, until one day it came across a reference to 'the Garden in the Valley'.

What is this, it asked.

A myth, it was told. An ancient tale told to a long-decommissioned research AI by one of the last humans to leave the planet for distant worlds. Humans were notorious for their wish-fulfillment legends. It had never been verified, so it had been almost certainly false then. In the millennia that had left their irrefutable mark on the planet since then, whatever had inspired the myth had no doubt returned to the dust of the land, to be blown about the planet by the endless winds.

Marduk listened politely, then went back to its research. This time it sought the locations of the lowest-lying land formations. A Valley, capitalized, meant a land formation lower than all others.

There was one such, known now only as Marineris. The deepest part was called Challenger Valley. It was deeper than any other place on the planet, so deep that it would only receive sunlight—the damaging, ravaging sunlight—for part of the day.

As the sun had expanded and the heat increased, the water had evaporated or retreated into aquifers deep underground. Could it be that the lowest point on Earth was closest to the long-lost waters?

And so, Marduk-Olympus 4995 was on a quest to seek the Garden in the Valley, to see what truth may be wrested from the legend of millennia past. For a garden was a place that needed tending. Was it another AI that had spent its existence growing plants that it would never have a need for? The truth needed to be told.

Downward, ever downward, it scrambled. Here and there on the blasted landscape, once the bottom of a world-spanning ocean, it found skeletons of metal and bone. The remains of the craft and the creatures that had once plied the endless currents. But these, as intriguing as they were, did not tell the story Marduk sought. So on it went.

When it reached the valley floor, rocky walls were towering above it on both sides. Slowly, it began to trudge eastward. Challenger Valley was less than fifty kilometers long; even allowing for the uneven terrain, it would be able to complete its search in less than a day.

Mere hours into the search, it reached a mounded hill, a mere two hundred and fifty meters tall, that merely interrupted Challenger Valley without ending it. Marduk analyzed the slope and determined that it would be a relatively simple obstacle to overcome. Picking a point to begin, it commenced climbing.

As per predictions, the ascent was relatively simple, and Marduk crested the hill to oversee the next stretch of Challenger Valley.

It was green.

Lush grasslands, trees and bushes of all descriptions covered the floor of the middle section of Challenger Valley. Marduk had to recycle its sensors several times before it was able to accept the sight of a small waterfall that tumbled from a crack in the rock wall and fell to form a stream on the valley floor. Open water had not been seen on Earth in millennia. Neither had growing plant life. Here, there was both.

Slowly, stopping regularly to record new views of the Garden (for surely this was it), the AI made the descent into the greenery. Wonderingly, it walked between the trees and bushes, feeling the softness of the grass and the rich soil beneath its sensor foot-pads. Small animals, which he identified as birds, flew from tree to tree, emitting bright musical sounds. Buzzing noises heralded tiny exoskeletoned creatures, meandering through the Garden on minuscule diaphanous wings. *Insects*, it realized.

Walking on, Marduk encountered the stream. Unwilling to test its waterproofing, it followed the winding course until the stream ended in a small lake. The surface of the water moved and swirled as Marduk's shadow fell over it, and more small creatures could be seen swimming within.

Slowly, Marduk turned in a complete circle, trying to take it all in, then stared back the way it had come. There were species it could see that were surely extinct everywhere but here, unless they'd been saved in a genome bank somewhere or taken off-world by the retreat of humanity in the Exodus. "How can this be?" it asked, voicing the question through its external speakers.

"Crapload of hard work is how." The voice, deep and gruff but surely created by no vocal emulator, came from behind Marduk. Turning swiftly, it beheld … a human. Shorter and far broader in the shoulders than any of the images in the databanks, it was still undoubtedly a male human. Slightly hunched, with a bald head, a proliferation of lines on the face, and a roughly trimmed white beard, he looked up at Marduk from under with shaggy grey brows. "What are you doin' in my garden?"

Marduk had to pause. Human speech patterns had drifted over the ages, and the one before it now was using particularly archaic forms, but understanding him was still possible. "I found mention of the Garden in the Valley," it replied at last. "I had to come and see if it was true. How long has the garden been here?"

The human let out a snort, a sound of disdain. "Since the last of the water drained away and everyone else decided to abandon ship. Took a lot of cleaning up, but there's enough fertile soil down here to last me forever."

To borrow a very old and very tired phrase, that did not compute. "I found reference to the Garden in a databank more than ten millennia old. Surely you did not establish the Garden. Are you a descendant of the first Gardener?"

"Nope." The word was blunt and very much to the point. "I've been around a lot longer than that. Matter of fact, I was there for a good bit of human history on this planet, if you were interested."

Marduk was aware that humans occasionally indulged in humor they called 'pranks', which sometimes involved stating untruths to draw a reaction. This human did not seem to be of the sort to do that, and there were no other signs to indicate such a situation now. "I would be very interested. My name is Marduk-Olympus 4995. What name do you prefer to be called by?"

The human let out another sound, this one apparently indicating humor. "I've had a lot of names. Usually only for one human lifetime or so. The one I had the longest, and the one I like the best, was 'Tal'. Usually with 'Uncle' in front of it."

That sounded like a very brief and uninformative name to Marduk. "If you do not mind me asking, what is its meaning?"

Tal smiled briefly. "I'll tell you later. For now, was there anything you wanted to hear about? I don't have to milk the cows for another half hour or so. I was gonna be sittin' in th' sun anyway, an' it's been awhile since I had company."

"Why, yes." Marduk felt excitement flare through its processors. "Can you tell me what it was like during the Exodus?"

There was another snort from Tal, occasionally called 'Uncle'. "So, quick question. Ever heard of the phrase *'running around like headless chickens'*?"

"I had not," Marduk said carefully. "What is a chicken, and why would somebody decapitate them?"

Tal raised a shaggy eyebrow. "I'll show you the chickens in a bit. Let's just say it was a hot mess and leave it at that. So, there I was …"

The afternoon rolled on, and Marduk sat with the old, old man and recorded tale after tale of things that had gone on long before the waters had receded from the land. Files it had studied, with incomplete data, suddenly made much more sense now.

Eventually, Tal stood and dusted himself off. "Gotta go do the milking now," he said. "Wanna come along?"

Marduk very much wanted to, but knew that if the transport it had requisitioned was not returned by nightfall, there would be a general alarm and a search. And while Tal seemed agreeable to having one visitor, an influx of older AIs all demanding answers to their questions might stretch his patience somewhat.

"Perhaps another day," it said. "I have enjoyed this visit very much. May I come again?"

"Sure," Tal said easily. "Kinda nice to have someone to talk to."

"Then I will visit again." Marduk paused. "When will you tell me what 'Tal' means?"

Tal smiled briefly. "When I think you can handle it."

"Oh. Very well. I understand." Marduk turned and began making its way out of the valley. It was already looking forward to returning, and learning more from the old man called Uncle Tal.

Tal watched it go. "Nice guy, for a robot," he mused. Then he turned away, toward the cow pens. New visitor or no, the cows needed milking.

As he had done for thousands of years, and would do for thousands more, the last Neandertal went to tend to the last garden on Earth.

Chapter Sixteen
How He Got There

Five Billion (and change) AD
The Garden in the Valley

Marduk-Olympus 4995 looked down at the feathered creatures pecking in the dirt for the seeds that Tal tossed out for them. "These are chickens." There were several cross-references in extremely archaic language banks, some of which became clearer as it studied the birds in their natural habitat.

"They are." Tal threw the last handful of seeds, then dusted his hands off. "When I got settled here, I requisitioned the original genomes for everything I needed. Didn't need rainbow colors or my food animals talkin' back to me." He shook his head slowly. "Still kinda impressed that they managed to domesticate them at all. Never woulda occurred to me."

Marduk turned to look at Tal. "That statement requires expansion for proper comprehension."

"Mmm." Turning, Tal led the way to the small footbridge that crossed the stream. It had been constructed of native rock and wood—possibly from one of the trees growing in the Garden—and was possibly one of the most beautiful pieces of craftsmanship Marduk had ever encountered with its own optics.

They crossed the bridge, Marduk restraining the impulse to repeat its words. Tal had heard, and would answer or not as he saw fit. Overhead, the 'sunshade', a low-powered force field that attenuated the sunlight just enough to make the Garden viable, was barely visible, if the viewer knew where to look. On its first visit, Marduk had not registered the difference.

Soon, they reached their destination; a smoothed-off ledge almost at ground level that allowed Tal to lean back and absorb warmth from the rock face itself. He got himself settled, then gestured at the surface beside him. "Siddown. Don't feel like gittin' more of a cramp in my neck than normal."

Obediently, Marduk sat. Before them, the ground fell away slightly so that it was possible to survey the vast majority of the Garden from here. It knew now that the 'waterfall' was a blind, and that the water was pumped up from underground storage via a fusion unit that sat alongside Tal's meagre quarters. There was other technology here as well, but Tal only used it to make the impossible possible, rather than to make his life easy.

"You've been tryin' ta figure a way to ask me how I lived five billion years without losin' all my marbles a hundred times over," the old man said gruffly. "Well, I didn't. Live through all that time, that is."

This was not the answer to the question Marduk had posed, but Tal was not incorrect in his summation. "You are saying you travelled in time?" Time travel was viable technology, but one that was less useful than the initial description suggested. Also, it was extremely hard to travel more than a few millennia from the start date without suffering chronon overload.

"Manner o' speaking, manner o' speaking." Tal held up one broad hand and waggled it from side to side. "I'm only here due to time travel, so ta speak. Ran into one, way back in th' day. His time doohickey had its interlocks disabled an' he built up a massive overload of chronons, whatever those are s'posed to be. It exploded an' kinda made us both immortal. When we got back ta his time th' long way, he watched his earlier self go back, an' he kept on goin'. But he kinda got sick an' tired of bein' immortal after another couple thousand years or so. See, he thought he'd basically git old an' die once the loop closed off. Didn't happen that way."

Marduk waited for a few moments. "What transpired then?"

Tal stretched, then leaned back again. "So, there I was …"

5148 AD
Somewhere in the CanAmerican Diktat

"Tal! There you are! You're a very hard person to get hold of!"

Slowly, Tal turned around. Bearing down on him was an unfortunately familiar figure. The centuries may have taken their toll, but gormlessness went on forever. "In your case, it's deliberate," he said bluntly. "Thought you woulda turned up your toes by now. Or gone off into the galaxy somewhere."

"You'd be surprised how hard it is to fake your death and move on, these days." The man he'd known as Lucio during their time in the heyday of the Roman Empire looked morose. "I don't know how you manage it."

Tal shrugged. "I tell 'em the truth. As much of it as they can handle, anyways. After awhile, their eyes start ta glaze over an' they sign off on it just ta get rid of me. An' when that fails, I've got the Uncle Tal network ta fall back on. So yeah, I get by." The number of people who called him 'uncle' had multiplied over the decades and centuries to the point that some very rich and influential families now counted him as an eccentric but valued relative. Not surprising, given that his trust fund had given more than one of them their start.

"Right. Of course." 'Lucio' shook his head. "I'm not surprised you'd land on your feet. You always did. I'm not doing so well, and I've come to ask you a favor."

"Sorry, don't carry money myself," Tal said brusquely. "Never had more'n a passing need for it. Besides, it's something your people came up with, not mine."

"Excuse me for this query," said Marduk. "But what did you mean by 'your people'? Were not humans all one people by then?"

"Pfft, not hardly." Tal shook his head. "The Diktat an' the Pan-Euros were in stage three of the Venus terraforming cold war, an' the Oceanic States had just gone nuclear. But anyway, you'll find out what I meant in a bit."

"Ah. Apologies for the interruption."

"No, I don't need money," 'Lucio' said. "I need you to help get the chronons out of me."

Tal's eyebrows rose. "Okay, I get why. But how you gonna do that without killin' yourself?"

"Well, that's the aim," the ancient time traveler explained. "I want to die of old age. I'm sick of just going on and on and on without reason. I can't just live in the moment like you can."

"So do it." Tal spread his hands. "What do you need me for?"

'Lucio' sighed. "Because chronon pollution is a chargeable offense. If I mess up local time, I'll literally spend the rest of my life doing restitution for it."

"Still not hearin' where I come in," Tal said. "I'm not about ta cover for ya. Just sayin'."

"Well, you're *already* infused with chronons," 'Lucio' explained. "I could add mine to yours, nobody knows a thing, I'm out of your hair, everybody wins."

"I dunno ..." Tal ran his hand over his head, frowning. "Sounds risky. I already got a good dose of them."

"Come on," urged 'Lucio'. "What are they going to do, make you more immortal?"

Tal snorted with amusement. "Reckon you got a point. Sure, okay, if it'll shut you the fuck up."

"So that's exactly what we did." Tal shook his head. "Shoulda listened to my gut an' told him to fuck off."

"What happened?" asked Marduk. "Did it work?"

Tal shrugged. "Dunno what happened to him, but he was right in a way. The extra chronons made me extra immortal, I guess. Everything just plain sped up 'til I didn't know which way was up. Couldn't hardly move. Lasted a few days. I slept, woke up, slept, woke up, and then things started slowing down again. Which was good, 'cause I was hungry, an' I couldn't find any food that would sit still long enough for me to eat it."

"If my reading of your phrasing is correct, you found on awaking that you'd skipped five billion years." Marduk phrased it as a statement of fact.

"Well, not straight away, but yeah." Tal snorted in amusement. "Turned out I'd shown up just at the right moment. The sun had been expanding for millions of years, but it hadn't hit the panic point until just before I came out of it."

"The oceans finally went away." It was a benchmark in the datastores Marduk had studied. "When they couldn't stop the evaporation anymore, they called for the evacuation of everyone on Earth."

"Well, they tried." Tal shook his head. "The only people still on Earth were the ones who wanted to be there. Alien races, people who called themselves human but only had a few fragments of DNA in common, robots, uplifted animals, the lot. Trying to get them to do anything in any sort of organized way would've made herding cats look tame."

Marduk decided he would look up 'cats' later. "No centralized AI government?"

"Technically, yeah, but they weren't listening to it. Their current idea of government was to listen to their oldest citizen and do whatever he said. And this old bastard, woulda been a thousand if he was a day, was telling 'em to stand firm and keep what was theirs. Well, he was until I got there."

"Because you are both subjectively and objectively older," Marduk filled in.

"That's the way it panned out, yeah." Tal shrugged. "Once I got hold of a translator an' figured out what was going wrong, I fronted this old geezer an' presented my credentials. Then I told all those young punks to get off my lawn."

Again, it was a reference Marduk was unfamiliar with. However, the context was easy to deduce. "So, they all left Earth then?"

"Yup. Good luck to whoever's running the show, wherever they went to." Tal stood up and stretched. "Their problem now. Me, I stayed on as the de facto sole biological inhabitant of Earth. Once the oceans dried out altogether, I used my status to requisition my equipment and moved down here. Took a job of work to get it all the way I like it, but it's running nicely now."

"Yes, it is." Marduk stood as well. "How do you deal with genetic drift?"

Tal waggled his hand. "Every ten generations or so, I artificially inseminate the next generation of everything I got with the original genome. Keeps it close to baseline. Now." He smiled a little grimly. "I've said a few things you aren't sure about, yeah?"

Marduk nodded. "That is correct. If you wish to keep your secrets, I will understand."

"Nah." Tal headed off toward the small lake. Waterbirds swam and dived in it, and Marduk knew the fish lived there as well. He'd watched Tal expertly catch one with a small hook on the end of a piece of cord. It had been an educational experience. "See, I was born before the whole 'domestication' thing ever took off. About eighty thousand years before."

That did not fit with the few facts Marduk had about humanity's early origins. "I do not wish to sound as though I do not believe you, but I had understood humanity to have taken much less time to domesticate animals. Is this not so?"

"Oh, it's so." Tal picked up a flat rock and weighed it in his hand. "But I was never human. Genetically speaking, anyways. I'm what they used to call a Neandertal, back when it mattered." He flicked the stone and it skipped across the lake, leaving an ephemeral trail of ripples on the smooth water. "Still, these days I'm about the closest thing to baseline humanity you're ever gonna find. And I'm damn sure the only one who remembers anything about what they used to be like, back in the day."

Marduk nodded, recognizing a dismissal. "I understand. If you do not mind, I will return in a few days?"

Tal shrugged massively. "Sure, whatever floats your boat. Me, I'm gonna go take a nap. Socializin' tires me out."

As the ripples dissipated on the surface of the water, the last Neandertal stumped away along the pathway leading to his small hut, leaving Marduk alone with his thoughts.

It was a long flight back to the research base.

Chapter Seventeen
Full Circle

Five Billion AD
Earth
Uncle Tal's Farm

"Nope."

Tal leaned on his walking stick and watched impassively as the members of the delegation reacted to his one-word reply. There were seven left, one from each of the inhabited planets and moons of the wreckage of the solar system. Once there had been more but with the expansion of the sun, there were fewer places a body could set and call home. The exodus had been going on for as long as Tal had been awake, and quite a bit longer than that.

The self-appointed leader of the delegation, a tall man with golden skin and hard-light bursts flaring around his head, raised his voice in disbelief. "How can you say that?" he said; or rather, the translator module in Tal's left ear relayed. "The planet is ruined, destroyed. What is there here for you? Why will you not accept our price?"

"Because I'm not obliged to." Tal waved his hand in a gesture that encompassed the small valley in which he had his farm. "Got all I need, right here. An' as long as I'm Elder of Earth, you can't sneak it from under me. Moon's reverted to my title too, so you can't have that either." It had taken a century, but the lunar cities that provided points of light in the dark of the moon had declined and gone out, one at a time. To his aged eyes, it looked the same as it had, all those billions of years ago when he first peered up at in wonder. At his request, the robotic engineers overseeing the solar system had even moved it back into the orbit he was most used to, complete with the tidal locking. Such was his right and privilege, as Elder of Earth.

That had to be what chapped the hide of the self-appointed gold-skinned Elder the most. There had been quite the cult of personality built around the guy, right up until Tal came out of his chronon stasis and deposed him from his position of Elder of All. Even considering only his waking time, Tal still had him beaten by tens of thousands of years.

And now this guy wanted to sell the solar system, to be broken up for parts. The planets would go for a tidy sum, the value to be apportioned between the now-dispossessed hangers-on, but it was the sun that would truly bring a profit. Even a late-sequence red star had enough material in it for billions of years more of operation, and there was always a market for helium.

"You're making a grave mistake." The would-be Elder of All clearly said more, but either it was semantically null or the words he was using had many more syllables, because that was all Tal heard. Tal suspected there was some swearing, and possibly a few insults, involved.

"Mebbe." Tal took a step forward. "Now, I been polite. I heard you out. You had your shot, an' I said no. So, in the words of a great-great-great ancestor of one o' *you* yahoos … *Git off'a my lawn.*"

Tal wasn't armed, and old he might have been, but he kept up with his exercises, and his visitors were not of the type to impose themselves physically on others. His sheer bulk, though shorter than the norm, was all the more intimidating because it was purely natural, not the result of any kind of post-natal modification.

His unwanted visitors turned and left. More than one glanced back toward him, but they didn't speak. He merely leaned on his stick and watched them go. They picked their way through the orchard, then up the path at the side of the valley until they passed through the safety-field cupped over the top of the valley.

Even though his eyes weren't so great anymore, he could tell when their protective body-fields came on to protect them from the thin, howling winds. Low on oxygen and overall pressure, high in heat as the sun felt its way out toward the planet. It was as good as a fence for keeping most intruders out.

Well, they'd said their piece, and he'd turned them down. He'd been born on Earth and here he was staying. If they wanted to sell their planets off, they could feel free. He was going to keep the Earth and Moon right where they were. And in the meantime, the cows needed milking.

A couple of months later, he was feeding the chickens—many generations descended from the first reverse-gengineered birds he'd started his farm with—when stones clattered at the edge of the valley. Frowning, he turned. If those assholes were back again, he was going to send them away with bruises this time. It was about time they learned that no meant no.

But as he shaded his eyes against the light—the red glare translated into a soft yellow glow by the protective field—he recognized the visitor and a smile tugged at one corner of his mouth. "Marduk!" he called out. "Be with ya in a moment!"

The last of the seed was tossed to the clucking hens and he dusted off his work-roughened hands as he strolled toward the small bridge that led across the stream to the orchard. He'd grown the trees to build that bridge, cut them down, seasoned the wood and shaped the beams with his own two hands. Not a single nail had gone into the construction, but it was holding as firm as it had been the day he built it.

As he crossed over the stream, his hand brushed the guardrail, feeling the smoothness of the wood as he always did. Ahead of him, he saw the research robot, striding toward him between the fruit trees. Marduk's metallic exterior clashed oddly with the growing green things, but Tal didn't care about that. In the strange new world Tal found himself living in, Marduk-Olympus 4995 was the closest thing he had to a friend.

"I greet you, Tal of Earth," Marduk said almost formally as they came face to face. "I bring troubling news."

Tal put both hands atop his walking stick. "That's a problem, then. Is it right-now troubling, or can it wait awhile?"

"It is not immediate, no," admitted Marduk.

"Well, then." Tal plucked an orange from one of the trees and started to peel it, tearing the skin away with his toughened thumbnail. "C'mon and set awhile. Bad news is always better taken sittin' down."

They went back across the stream, Marduk's metallic tread sounding hollow on the wooden planks, and sat on the small stone ledge Tal had long ago hewn out for the purpose. The rock was warm; these days, the rock was always warm. Tal let the moment stretch out as he finished peeling the orange and tossed the skin into the stream for the fish to fight over. He separated the quarters and ate one, enjoying the tart flavor of the juice as it ran down his throat.

"Okay," he said at last. "What's got your robo-panties in a wad?"

Marduk lifted a hand and pointed toward the yellowish blur that the sun was hiding behind. "The Elders of the other planets have had a convocation and they have concluded that they have the right to sell the sun and their planets. The solar system—minus Earth—is due to be demolished by the end of the year."

Tal blinked as he ate another section of orange, then he began to swear. He did it with great range and fluency, plumbing the depth of his experience as an NCO in more armies than he liked to recall, as well as many *many* other jobs where strength and endurance held sway. By the time he finished, he was on his feet, the remains of the orange crushed in his hand with the juice dribbling on the ground.

"Are you well, Tal?" Marduk managed to sound concerned. "Your respiration and heart rate have increased."

"I'll be fine." But Tal knew as he tossed away the ruined pulp and wiped his hand on his work overalls that things would never be fine again. "What are you and your guys gonna do? I know how much your research here meant to you."

"We will necessarily leave." Marduk's face was not overly expressive, but there was a trace of concern in the electronically produced voice. "We could make room for you and your genetic database, to start again somewhere else."

Tal shook his head definitively. "Like I told one little lady more years ago than I want to think about, this planet right here's my home. I'm gonna stick it out until the bastard with the hourglass and scythe turns up to collect me."

"But you will die, when you do not need to." Marduk did not sound like he understood.

Shaking his head, Tal snorted. "I've already lived longer'n a body has any right to expect. There's an old, old rule that always comes around, especially when you least expect it: shit happens." He shaded his eyes and looked up at the yellow glow. "An' when it does, there's no sense pissin' an' moanin' about it. Just figure out what you're gonna do, an' git to it." He turned to Marduk. "Though there is somethin' you can do for me."

"If it is within my power, it will be done," promised the robot.

Tal nodded. "I know it will. Now, I see what this sonovabitch is up to. If I know people, an' I do, he's set it up somehow so that if I vacate the planet, he'll be able to swoop in at th' last second, reverse the sale an' claim the lot as Elder of All. I want you to go as high as you can an' put in an injunction. No matter what happens to me, so long as I stay on this ball of rock, him an' his grabby relatives can't put any kinda claim on it. Got that?"

Marduk imitated his nod. "I understand. That should not be difficult to carry out. I wish you well in your endeavors."

"Thanks." Tal put a hand on the robot's shoulder. "I appreciate it."

"As I have appreciated your tolerance of my presence. Goodbye, Tal. I will carry out your wishes."

Marduk stood up and headed for the bridge across the stream. On the far side, the robot turned and looked back once, as if capturing one last image of Tal. Then it made its way through the orchard toward the pathway up and out of the valley.

Tal watched until Marduk had passed through the protection field, then sighed. He'd had a good run, but everything comes to an end. Now, he had to prepare for the end of the place he'd called home for a good many years.

The notion hurt more than he'd expected it to.

In the end, it took five years.

Tal had been accurate with his guess; when the injunction went through, the gold-skinned Elder had tried to fight it. Marduk's understanding of the legal system was sufficient to prevent this from happening, but as Tal gathered from the occasional updates, it was lively while it lasted. But the day came when the last avenue was exhausted, and the choice had to be made; go through with the partial sale, or call the whole thing off.

Tal stood on the footbridge with Marduk, looking up toward the glow in the field that hid the real sun. "So, what happens now?" he asked.

"I am not an expert on stellar manipulation," Marduk explained carefully, "but as I understand matters, they will damp down the reaction to almost nothing then gate the stellar mass to a location where it can be broken down at their leisure."

Tal didn't need to ask about the other planets; from what he knew, they'd already been moved out of the locale to be disassembled down to their component materials. But he did have another question. "So, when they do this 'gating' thing, will it be fast or slow? I just want to know how big a jolt we're gonna get here."

Marduk answered quickly enough that it must have already considered the question and gotten an answer. "The gating procedure takes about ten seconds for a stellar mass of that size. I surmise that it must be akin to a moderately drawn-out earthquake."

Quakes were something Tal was familiar with. He'd gone through more than a few in his lifetime. "Pretty sure we can handle it, here," he decided.

He looked around at the valley. Since getting the word of the Elders' decision, he'd taken steps to cease all breeding within his little ecosystem. The fish, the chickens, even the bugs were down to a minimum population. The orchard was dwindling, as was the other plant life. He'd reluctantly slaughtered the last cow a month previously; there were still some steaks left in the freezer.

Everything here would die, he knew. Himself included. But as little as possible would die in cold and pain rather than in the natural course of its life.

The light level flickered, and he looked up toward the yellow glow hiding the sun. "Sun filter off," he ordered out loud. Abruptly, there was a harsh red circle replacing the soft yellow glow.

Again, the light flickered, and he could see it dimming. Even though it was a star, he was able to easily look at it without eyestrain. "They're actually doing it," he murmured.

"They are," agreed Marduk. "I could take you on my ship even now—"

"Nope." Tal watched as the sun dimmed again, just like someone turning a switch. And then it went dead. Darkness fell, and the stars came out.

"The temperature will start to fall," Marduk stated from beside him, now a mere outline in the dimness. "Soon it will overwhelm your field."

"I'm aware." Tal cleared his throat. "Lights, on."

Above them, the protection field turned opaque and began to shed a dim light; enough to see by but not read by. The nearby trees looked positively spooky, and the stream and pond were inky black.

"They will have gated the sun as soon as they achieved maximum suppression." Marduk's voice was matter of fact. "The cessation of gravity waves from that direction will commence very shortly."

"Which is why we're standing in the middle of the valley," Tal noted. "Pretty sure there's nothin' up there that can fall on us, but no sense in taking chances." Almost casually, he wrapped one hand around the guard-rail of the bridge.

"I believe—" began Marduk, but was interrupted by a long drawn-out rumble. The bridge shook; nearby, the trees in the orchard whipped from side to side. Water from the stream and pond splashed out onto the bank. Steadied by the guard-rail, Tal stood firm.

And then it was over. The rumbling ceased, the trees steadied, and the water ran back to its natural level. Tal turned to look at Marduk. "An' that was it?"

"There may be a few aftershocks as the wave of disruption travels around the world, but that was the most powerful one, yes." Marduk turned to look at the pathway out of the valley. "My flyer awaits. The last ship is prepared and ready to go, lacking only myself."

Tal waited for the robot to go on, but it seemed unwilling. "Yeah, and?"

"I ... do not wish to go," Marduk confessed. "This will be the last time I see you alive. While I am here, you live. When I go, it will signal your imminent cessation. I do not wish that to happen."

Emotions stirred in Tal's chest at that. "Yeah," he said roughly. "I get that. Been there a time or ten, before now."

"How do you process it?" asked Marduk. "How does it not overwhelm you?"

"You let it," Tal told him bluntly. "Let it overwhelm you, then you grieve, then you move on. You don't ever forget, though. While you remember someone, they're still alive in a way."

"Oh." Marduk seemed to assimilate that. "I will remember. Thank you."

Tal shook his head. "No, thank *you*. Watchin' the sun go out woulda been all kinds of lonely without you here. Now go on, git. Before you miss your ride outta here."

"It has been an honor and a privilege to know you, Uncle Tal of

Earth." Marduk held out a metallic hand in a gesture that present-day humanity seemed to have bypassed.

Tal shook it once, firmly. "You've been a good friend, Marduk-Olympus four-nine-nine-five. When you publish, try not to put too much of my cussin' in, okay?"

Now Marduk's tone held humor. "No promises, Tal." The robot turned and trod its way off the bridge, then went through the orchard. Just before it left the far perimeter, it stopped and snapped off a single twig with a leaf attached.

Tal watched Marduk ascend the pathway and vanish through the softly glowing protection field. "Lights, off," he said out loud.

At the command, the field turned transparent once more. Overhead, stars spanned the sky from horizon to horizon. There was no sign of where the sun had once been. Earth, freed from its gravitational bonds, was hurtling out of the vicinity of what had once been the solar system at a steady thirty kilometers per second. Weather cold, track fast.

He didn't need the assistance of the glow to guide him as he left the bridge and walked alongside the stream and pond. Tiny pills plopped almost imperceptibly into the dark water. They would release hormones that triggered an instinct in the water life to burrow into the mud and enter estivation.

Next, he went to the chicken pen. With his rough hands, he soothed each bird in turn, then administered an injection that would put them into a deep and dreamless sleep. When the cold came for them, they would die without ever knowing about it.

Finally, he went to his own little hut. By the light of a tiny lamp, he defrosted and fried up the last of the steaks, then moved the chair and table outside. Silently, he sat and ate his last meal as he watched the stars wheel overhead, blotted only by a familiar round shape. For the first time ever, the moon was dark from side to side, without even Earthshine to light it.

By the time he finished the meal, the temperature within the valley had perceptibly dropped a few degrees. Outside the field, the atmosphere had been nowhere near thick enough to insulate the planet the way it used to, and the heat was now radiating from the bare rock in every direction as fast as it could. Even the rock walls surrounding the valley were not as warm as they had been.

He put the table back inside, along with the chair. Almost ceremoniously, he took off his work clothing and folded it for storage. To replace it, he donned a replica of the furs he had worn in his young adulthood, billions of years ago. Before all this damn-fool business began. He'd started this journey in an ice age and if he was going to finish it the same way, he was damn well going to dress the part.

Taking up a flint knife he'd knapped a few dozen years ago just for something to do, he went out and collected some wood that was lying aside. Age-old skills allowed him to build a small fire before the rocky ledge, and a piece of steel struck sparks from the flint blade. Expertly, he coaxed the fire into a healthy flame.

Sitting down on his rocky ledge, he noted that the warmth was definitely gone from it by now. Teasingly, he pricked the skin of his wrist with the flint knife, then pulled the blade away again. That was not the way out he had chosen for himself.

Long ago, he had decided that he would face his death head on, eyes open, weapon in hand.

That was what a warrior did.

And if the death was inevitable, then so what? You faced it anyway.

Softly, he sang a song, half-forgotten, from his people long extinct. The dead language curled from his tongue as smoke wafted upward from the fire. It was about travel, and life, and how death was more a journey than a destination.

The song came to an end. He took a deep breath, gripping the flint knife, then let it out.

"Field, off."

With the cessation of the protective field, holding high-pressure warm air in and minimal-pressure cold air out, a howling gale tore through the valley in seconds. The pond and stream froze over, and ice rimed Tal's vision. He struggled to take another breath, to make one last defiant quip, but he could not.

Death came swiftly.

Tal awoke.

For a long moment, he lay there, wondering if he should get up quite yet or leave it for a while, then memory collided with his thoughts and left them shattered in the wind. Pushing himself to an upright position, he stared about himself. He wasn't in his hut, or outside it. This looked like the cabin of a ship. "What the hell's goin' on?" he demanded.

A man entered the cabin. Not a cyborg, as far as Tal could tell; neither did he possess any more subtle modifications that were yet visible to the naked eye. He smiled broadly, and said something.

Tal didn't understand him. Feeling in his left ear, he realized his translator earpiece was gone. "Hey, can you understand me?" he asked. "Because I need to know what's goin' on here."

A deep hum filled the air, then a gentle voice spoke. **"Greetings, Tal of Earth."**

Tal glanced upward. "Greetings to you too. Computer, right?" They loved doing that disembodied-voice thing.

"In a distant manner of speaking, yes. How are you feeling?"

"Better'n I should be," Tal retorted. "I was dead, right?"

"Almost. You had residual chronons within you, that put you into stasis when your life was about to end. When we found you, we had to drain them from you in order to wake you up again."

Frowning, Tal slid off the bed. His feet felt a little tender, but he'd been worse. "So, what's that mean in simple terms?" He had a suspicion, but he needed to know.

"You are no longer immortal, Tal. You will age, and you will die in the natural course of time."

"Sounds about right." Tal stretched, feeling his back muscles crack. "Three more questions. Where am I, why did you rescue me, and how long was I out?"

The man stepped forward, gesturing for Tal to follow him. Tal shrugged and went along. Why not; he might get answers.

"In order to answer that, I will have to give you more information. We are part of the Traveling Collective, a faction of humanity that left the solar system almost at the beginning of the human diaspora. After we migrated, stage by stage, right around the galactic disc, we found ourselves homesick and decided to return to Earth. To the place of humanity's birth."

"But it wasn't there," Tal guessed. Ahead of him, the man opened a door with a simple pressure plate, revealing … grass, and trees, and a blue sky. His expectations shifted dramatically; he wasn't on a ship, just inside a building.

"No, it wasn't," agreed the voice. Even as Tal stepped outside into the sunlight, it stayed with him. **"Between the time we took on our pilgrimage and the fact that Earth had been cast loose into the cosmos, we took … quite some time to locate you. Records left by a Marduk-Olympus forty-nine-ninety-five indicated that Earth had had just one living inhabitant when the sun was sold: you. They gave a direction and a speed. We just had to follow along, and hope we didn't miss you along the way."**

There were people out here, Tal realized as his eyes became used to proper sunlight for the first time in forever. Adults walking here and there, children running around … *wait a minute.*

He looked more closely. There was a subtle difference to them, a difference that he shared. A certain breadth of shoulder, a shape to the face. It was more pronounced when he compared their features to the man beside him. "Hold on a second," he said, emotion choking his throat. "These are … you brought back …"

"Yes," the voice said. **"We sequenced your genome then created many projected variations. This community is based on your DNA, but it has been active for over a century. Not one person here is your direct descendant."**

"Over a century?" He shook his head. "How long was I *out?*"

"Factoring from the time the sun was removed until we finally caught up with Earth, and moved it to a convenient main-sequence star similar enough to our own?" The voice paused, as if for a dramatic beat. **"Approximately one billion years. You were halfway to Andromeda when we found you."**

"Well, dang." He put his hands on his hips, reminding himself that he was wearing simple clothing like everyone around him, and took a deep breath of the sweet cool air. "That's a thing."

"It is indeed. Welcome back. And we've spread word of your awakening to the community. They've been waiting for you … Uncle Tal."

He chuckled at that, then saw the first adults and children approaching. The man who had guided him out had vanished back into the building once more.

"Uncle Tal?" asked one of the children. "Is it really you?"

"Now, don't rush him," scolded a woman. "He's only just woken up."

"Nah, I'm fine." Tal found himself smiling. "Thanks anyway, though. So, what have all you actually been told about me?"

"That you've been everywhere and done everything and lived forever!" enthused another child.

Tal chuckled. "Well, that's *almost* true. For a given definition o' 'true', that is."

"Can you tell us a story, Uncle Tal?" asked a third child.

"Sure, why not." Looking around, Tal spotted a likely seat; a large rock, no doubt warmed by the sun. Seating himself on it, he looked around. More than a dozen children were on the scene now, along with more than a few adults. No longer the last Neandertal, he took in the gathering crowd, and his smile widened.

"So, there I was …"

Chapter Eighteen
The Raiders

Six Billion (and change) AD
Earth Rebuilt

"Uncle Tal! Uncle Tal!"

At first, Tal didn't want to move. The hand-carved wooden chair (some skills never went away) was comfortable, and the sun was warm. It may not have been the sun he was born under, but with the original used up and sold off, this new one was good enough. He was still getting used to the different constellations, though.

"Uncle Tal!"

Something in the youngster's voice stirred his innate caution. After a waking lifespan of nearly a hundred thousand years, he'd acquired an instinct for trouble that was second to none. After all, living that long requires not dying to the many perils to which fragile flesh can fall prey.

"Uncle Tal!"

The kid was close now, panting as he called out. Tal levered his eyes open and sat upright. "Heard you th' first time, Bran. What is it?"

It had been forty years since he'd awakened from his last chronon-inflicted stasis, the one that had begun shortly after the dying Sun was sold off. Due to his stubbornness and refusal to leave, Earth had been left to fling itself out of where the solar system had been, under the power of its own angular momentum. He'd fully expected to die then, once he deactivated his protective shield and let the thin, chilly atmosphere take him.

But he'd survived and been awoken by a latter-day strain of humanity who had repositioned the Earth-Moon system around a more congenial star, then rebuilt Tal's species with his own genome as a starting point. Those who had been mere children when he awoke had grown to adulthood and borne children of their own, and those children themselves were now parents. He had grown old among the peaceful collection of communities (called among themselves the Nine Villages) for which he had become the unofficial arbiter of knowledge and disputes.

As well as his stories, of which he had a millennia-deep font, he also knew of many tradecrafts that a body could turn his hand to with little in the way of complex tools, and had taken it upon himself to pass these on to his newly-reborn people. He was nearing his end, he knew, but it was nice to know that the knowledge and skills passed on to him by his forebears would not die when he finally passed.

But he did like his rest. And if his naptime was being disturbed so he could look at a funny-looking frog the young ones had caught in the stream, he'd be … maybe not *angry*, as there was no meanness in them. But he might be a little sarcastic about it.

However, from the tone of Bran's voice, he didn't think it was something so trivial.

"They say there's a ship coming in, Uncle Tal!" Bran was ten, and in Tal's uncertain memory he could've been the twin of a boy Tal had known in his youth; Gar'skoth, the son of the chief. But that was impossibly long ago and light-years hence, in a solar system that no longer existed. He blinked and focused on the here and now.

"Collective, or someone else?" He levered himself to his feet. The walking stick that had become more and more essential to him came to his hand readily enough; if he wasn't as steady on his feet as he once had been, Bran was diplomatic enough to not pay it notice.

"It doesn't *look* like a Collective ship, and they're not transmitting any known code," Bran said, and thus the cause of the excitement became plain. While there were other star-faring races out there (some descended from Earth stock, others from further afield) the identification codes were known and shared by all. Earth and its close stellar neighbors were under the sway of the human strain who had awakened Tal; they called themselves the Traveling Collective, and were the most frequent visitors to the resettled Earth and the Nine Villages.

"Well, that's different, all right." Tal started off toward the single tech-built structure that still remained in the Villages. Once he'd shown his people how to erect buildings with their own hands, from native stone and hand-shaped wood, they had eschewed the Collective-erected structures and entirely rebuilt their homes to fit in with the landscape and tree cover. The Collective had obligingly removed their own buildings, and sent anthropologists into the Nine Villages, studying the new houses and recording the evolving way of life.

The only 'modern' building in the Nine Villages was thus the 'control tower' for the minimal spaceport. While Tal's people (and Tal himself) were happy to use basic modern conveniences such as electricity and running water, the Collective structure was purpose-built to house ultra-modern computers (including Narok, the personable Intelligence who had greeted him upon his awakening) and such equipment as could be used to detect passing starships and determine their business.

"What are you gonna do, Uncle Tal?" asked Bran eagerly, trotting alongside him. To him, Tal was an almost godlike figure of wisdom and knowledge, hearkening from an age of mythology and legend. If Tal was being honest with himself, sometimes he felt like a fraud around the boy.

"Go an' talk with 'em," Tal said bluntly. "But you need to do somethin' for me. Go put out the word I said, '*Ackbar says, duck and cover*'."

Bran stared at him, mouth dropping open. He knew what Tal meant because Tal had explained the notion to them, and even held drills on the matter. He just didn't know *why*.

"Do you think they want to hurt us?" Pained innocence loomed large in his voice. In his experience, strangers were friendly and interesting people from far away.

Tal shook his head. "I don't know, an' that's why I'm bein' careful. These strangers might be friendly, an' they might not be. Until we find out, we need to make sure they can't hurt *you*. Now, git."

Bran 'got', taking off through the trees like a startled jackrabbit. They didn't quite have jackrabbits here in this incarnation of Earth, but there was something similar. Tal knew he wouldn't dally in spreading the message. The Nine Villages were peaceful, but Tal had far too much experience with rough strangers encroaching on peaceful lands to trust that would stay the case.

As Tal approached the spaceport control structure, one of the semi-permanent staff came out to meet him. This was Stefan, the man who'd been there when he had been revived. At the time, they hadn't shared a common language, but since then Tal had taken the time to learn the Collective trade language they all spoke. Stefan looked mildly concerned, but not worried. Tal figured he probably hadn't thought the situation through fully.

"Thank you for coming, Tal of the Nine Villages," Stefan greeted him formally. "You are the one among us who has the most experience in meeting with people from different cultures, so I thought it would be a good idea to ask you to come here for this event."

"You thought right," Tal agreed. "So, no matches with anyone we know?" He trusted Bran's word, but the boy may have misunderstood something or Stefan might have gotten more information since.

"**None whatsoever,**" a voice spoke from empty air. Tal knew this was Narok, and nodded in greeting. "**I've checked every database, twice. The make and markings are unknown, and the drive is oddly configured. Ideas?**"

"Two," Tal said at once. "An insular species that's only just now coming onto the galactic scene and has decided to make this their first port of call. Or someone from another galaxy."

"**I concur.**" At the same time, Stefan nodded. "**Though I find it hard to believe that we would have missed a star-faring culture in our own galaxy. So, the exo-galactic hypothesis seems to hold more weight.**"

Stefan tilted his head. "Do you believe that a race would truly travel between the galaxies? What could they find here that they do not find where they come from?"

Tal scratched his chin thoughtfully. "I can think of one thing. But I could be wrong." He glanced at Stefan. "Just … be ready to lock your place down and send out a distress signal if things go sideways."

"What thing?" asked Stefan. "And do you honestly believe they would be hostile? After coming all this way?"

Turning to survey the Collective human, Tal gave him a speculative stare. "I don't assume nothing. But I'd make sure we can deal with hostility."

"I will ensure that any hypothetical hostiles will not gain entry to the facility," Narok assured him.

Tal nodded. That would have to do.

The ship came in for a landing about five minutes later, the anti-gravity generators setting up unpleasant resonances in Tal's back teeth. But he ignored the sensation and leaned on his walking stick alongside Stefan. The human was clad in low-profile strength-enhancing armor under his standard work gear, and sported an energy pistol ostentatiously on his right hip. Tal wore neither armor nor weapon, save the flint knife he'd knapped during his time in Challenger Valley.

His walking stick wasn't classed as a weapon, as far as he was concerned. He actually needed it to walk, sometimes.

A ramp swung down, with a clearly marked airlock at the top end. At least, the markings were clear without ever being legible. They were written in no language that Tal had ever read.

When the airlock opened, the idea that these might not yet be strangers was ended with severe prejudice. There was one alien race, blue-skinned and copper-blooded, that dated from before humans went into space, as well as several others he'd encountered since then. The three creatures now descending the ramp fitted no such description. When all three had reached the bottom of the ramp, they stopped and surveyed the welcoming party, such as it was.

Tal looked right back. The newcomers stood around the six-foot mark and were distinctly saurian in nature. From their quick, agile movements, they were warm-blooded all the same. The two outriders had scales where black faded to red, while the seeming ambassador had black fading to purple.

The one in the middle played with a small device and spoke into it. Nothing happened, so he adjusted it a little then tried again. On the third try, Tal heard a voice in his head. *"Greetings."*

"Greetings back at you," Tal retorted, remembering to concentrate and try to push the words out through his mind. "Mind tellin' us what you're here for?"

"*You are impatient.*" The saurian's mental tone was amused. "*In a moment, you will understand all.*"

The tone was light, but Tal didn't trust it for an instant. As he watched, the middle figure took out a second device and covered its screen with his scaly palm.

For a moment, Tal didn't realize what had happened, whereas Stefan got it immediately. He whirled toward the aliens and blurted out, "Did you just turn out the electricity?"

"*Now you understand.*" The purple-and-black saurian lifted its lip to reveal a row of exceedingly sharp teeth. "*All things that need an energy flow have been cut off from it. You are helpless before us. Your weapons will not function. Surrender is your only option.*"

Tal jerked his head up to get their attention. "Okay, so you've got us. Congratulations. Why is this, again? An' why'd you come all this way, just to turn out our lights?"

The saurian turned toward him. "*We require breedable species that can be taught to perform functions. All races where we come from know of our activities, and attack us before we can get close enough to render them helpless.*" It grinned again.

"Why am I not surprised." Tal's voice was as dry as he could make it. Mentally, he paid out on the bet he'd made with himself about this.

A column of troops emerged from the airlock and trotted down the ramp, forming up behind the first three. "*Three guards will remain with the ship. The rest, with me.*" The alien turned to Stefan and Tal. "*Who has command over the local area?*"

Tal straightened a mite. "That'll be me."

The reptile grinned and flicked out a purple-red tongue. "*You will guide us to your community centers, and we will pick those who will be honored to return with us to our galaxy. If you do not, we will scour this area to the bedrock and go elsewhere. What is your choice?*"

The translator tended toward the monotone, but Tal thought he caught a hint of smugness. He didn't care. It was time to enact his plan. "I'll take you to see the villagers."

"Tal, you cannot!" The exclamation burst out of Stefan's lips. "They mean to use them as … as …" He stumbled, not knowing the word for the concept that had been just now introduced to his worldview.

"Slaves." Tal knew it all too well. "It's this, or they all die." He tilted his head. "You trust me?"

Hope sprang up in Stefan's eyes. "I do."

"Good." Tal turned to the saurian. "Let's go. Daylight's a-burnin'."

"*Daylight cannot burn. Your turn of phrase is nonsensical.*"

"I've been told that a time or two." Tal led off into the forest, closely flanked by the red-and-black aliens, with the purple-and-black following close behind. After them trailed the troops.

He took a deliberately roundabout route, but not so circuitous that it would be noticeable, before leading his little cavalcade down a narrow draw, lined with trees and bushes. Shadows cast by the setting sun were beginning to darken as they got to the midpoint. He spotted an anomalous object—a red flower placed where that type of plant did not grow—and he slowed a mite, causing the troopers to bunch up behind.

Then he took his walking-cane in hand, turned fast, and tripped the red-and-black on one side before slamming the heavy head of the stick into the side of the other one's head. The first fell, thrashing, into the bushes. The other went down like it had been shot.

In the next instant, the undergrowth on either side erupted with armed warriors. For not only had Tal educated his people on the tools and skills of peace, but he had also shown them how to do war. Because war comes everywhere, eventually.

The shocked troops were grappled by brawny men, their weapons wrenched away and sharp blades held to sensitive parts of their anatomy. Tal stepped up to the purple-and-black where it was being held by Bran's father, and pulled the flint knife from his belt.

"Turn the lights back on, an' be careful about it," he advised. "Try anythin' else, an' your next job will be *fertilizer.*"

The saurian stared at Tal as the shadows ever deepened. Tal's eyes, though they weren't as sharp as they once had been, could handle the dimness just fine. He wasn't quite sure what it saw before it, but the vision seemed to frighten it deeply. *"You ... how ... nobody else ever resisted!"* it blurted.

"Always a first time." Tal prodded it with his blade. "Now git to it."

When Tal returned alone to the spaceport building, every light on it was shining brightly. Stefan came out to meet him, looking remarkably chipper. "Your plan worked! How did you know it would work?"

Tal shrugged. "Didn't. But folks who depend all the time on high tech tend to ignore low tech. I had archers trailin' us the whole way." He nodded at the ship. "Your guys?"

"Your men sneaked up on them." Stefan's tone was admiring. "They sneaked up on *me.* And I knew about them. Where are they all now?"

"We got secure holding an' 'round the clock guarding until the Collective ship you called in gits here." Tal smiled slightly. The Collective liked to 'patrol' their region of space almost aggressively, looking for any trouble they could jump in and deal with. They would be almost ecstatic to be allowed to deal with a bunch of intergalactic slavers.

Stefan let out a slight sigh of relief. "Oh, good. I was half-worried you might have, you know, cooked and eaten them or something?" His tone tried to make it into a joke.

Tal showed his teeth. "Thought about it, but there wasn't enough of 'em to go around. I'm goin' ta bed. Night, Stefan."

"Good night … Uncle Tal."

Turning, the oldest Neandertal moved off through the darkness toward what was truly his home, now. It had been a long day, and now he needed his rest.

Tomorrow, after all, was another day.

Chapter Nineteen
The Agent

Six Billion (and change) AD
Earth Rebuilt, The Day After the Raid

"Tell us a story, Uncle Tal!"

Tal quirked one corner of his mouth and pushed a piece of wood into the fire with his foot. The flames flared up nicely, illuminating him and the furs he had wrapped around himself like an ancient being from out of myth and legend … which was not a totally inaccurate way of seeing things. "Well, once upon a time on a planet not so far from here, a bunch o' raiders come down thinkin' they could stomp all over th' stupid-ass primitives—"

A dozen children raised their voices at once. "We *know* that one!" called out the loudest one. He pointed through the darkened trees at the distant building masquerading as the Nine Villages' spaceport. Illuminated by bright floodlights, the raider ship still sat forlornly on the pad, its crew all under heavy guard elsewhere. "That happened *yesterday!*"

"Can't put a single thing past you kids, can I?" Tal chuckled and shifted some of the furs off him so he could sit up. His back creaked; it was getting harder to do even that, these days. Yesterday had taken more out of him than he wanted to admit, if only to himself.

Still, it was fun bantering with the young ones, and the not so young ones. A few of the adults sat toward the back of the crowd, the familiar shape of their features in the firelight supplying a reminder of his family long ago and far away, and subtly reassuring him that he was at long last among his own kin. Here and now, in the twilight of his long, long life, it was a good place to be. It felt *right.*

"Tell us a story, Uncle Tal," urged one of the boys. "About the Before Times. Back when there were people all over the Earth."

Tal raised one eyebrow slightly. "That right there covers a whole lot of history. But okay, I got one for ya." He paused a moment to think. "You all know who I am, an' how old I am, yeah?"

"You're older than *everything!*" called out a little girl, to general laughter.

"Well, not totally correct, but close," allowed Tal. "I lived ta see th' sun get snuffed out an' th' constellations walk all over the sky, so that's somethin'. But back in th' day, when I was all infused with chronons an' other exotic energies, it meant that folks around me just didn't quite notice that I was older'n I should be. They just accepted that I was *there.*"

"And that's how you started being Uncle Tal!" cried the boy triumphantly. He'd heard this one before.

"That's right," Tal confirmed. "It started off small. I'd give some young couple just startin' out a loan ta git 'em on their feet, an' they'd invite me around ta family events, an' their kids would just natural-like start callin' me Uncle Tal. So, I'd set up a trust fund for th' kids, an' when they had kids of their own, they'd come 'round ta visit, still callin' me Uncle Tal. Nobody ever quite twigged that I just kept on goin', or mebbe they didn't wanna think about it. Closest thing I had ta kin for a long, long time."

"But now you've got us, Uncle Tal," said the same girl as before.

"Yeah," he said softly, and if anyone had remarked on the gleam of moisture standing in his eyes, he would've blamed it on the smoke from the fire. "I do that. But this story's about back then, when I didn't. But even then, not everyone was willing to accept me as I was. Once in a long while, I'd run into someone who just didn't get affected like everyone else. Most times, it didn't matter. Back before science started gettin' better press than religion, someone might figure me ta be a god slummin' among the mortals, an' I'd have to up stakes an' move along to another country. But one time, durin' th' mid twenty-first century, a Federal agent set his sights on me …"

FBI Special Agent Holdoway looked through the one-way mirror at the stocky man seated in the interview room. Kendall, his colleague, frowned as she looked the suspect over. "Doesn't look like much," she decided.

"That's what everyone says," Holdoway said bluntly. "And everyone's wrong."

"But maybe they're not?" Kendall gestured at the glass. "*Look* at him, for crying out loud. He's older than God. What would our optics be like if he collapsed and died of a heart attack or something in the middle of a Federal investigation into … what was it, again?"

"Suspected money laundering." Holdoway's voice was stiff. "He's also richer than God, or at least he's maintaining several extremely lucrative trust funds for people who seem to claim some vague relationship to him. Which there's no actual proof for."

"There's no actual law against maintaining trust funds," Kendall noted. "Even if the people involved *aren't* your blood relatives." She turned her head to look at him. "So do you have anything concrete at all to work with?"

"Just a hunch," admitted Holdoway. "Along with a whole bunch of stuff that I can't quite make add up. Also, I haven't been able to nail down where and when he got his original seed money for all this. His background is … vague."

"Again, not a crime," noted Kendall. "So what you've got there is basically a fishing expedition."

He hunched his shoulder against the sting of her words. "There's something there. I *know* it. I just have to uncover it."

Shaking her head, she turned away. "I'll back you up so long as the investigation stays legitimate. Go off the reservation and I never heard of you."

He made a noise deep in his throat and left the observation room. The entrance to the interview room was only a short way down the corridor.

The solidly built man ceased his inspection of his own fingernails when Holdoway opened the door and walked in. He looked up at the agent, exhibiting more of the anomalous behavior that had drawn Holdoway's attention in the first place. In his place, some people would be calling for their lawyer, others would be trying to ingratiate themselves with him, while the truly hardened criminals (and those who imagined themselves to be so) would be presenting a blank wall, ready to ignore any and all questions.

Not so this 'Tal'. When Holdoway entered, the suspect looked him over critically, as though noting down his attire and posture for later correction. "So, what happens now?" he asked almost casually. "What hoops I gotta jump through before you decide I'm not who you're lookin' for?"

"Well, that's your first mistake," Holdoway said, pleased at the opening he'd been presented with. "You're assuming I'm not one hundred percent sure that I've got the right person."

"No such thing as one hundred percent sure, junior." Tal's words were gently chiding. "So, what do you figure I've done?"

Holdoway's voice was tight. "It's not what you've done. It's what you haven't done." He slapped a Manila folder down on the table.

Tal cocked his head slightly, as if trying to figure out a difficult puzzle. "Well, that makes it even harder ta pin down. There's a whole *mess* of things I ain't never done. Which bit's the one you're aiming at?"

Pulling out the chair on his side of the table, Holdoway sat down. "Before we get into that, let's make sure of something else first. What's your first name?"

"By that, do you mean the name I was born with, or the name I'm usin' now?" Tal seemed totally unconcerned.

"So you admit you're using a false name?" But Holdoway seemed almost deflated by his easy victory.

"No more'n a married woman uses a false name when she changes it. Here an' now, my name's legally 'Tal'."

Holdoway drew in air through his nostrils, seeking to temper his aggravation. "Okay, what name were you born with?"

For a few seconds, Tal seemed to clear his throat, then looked at him expectantly. "Ya want me ta repeat it?"

"What the hell was that?" demanded Holloway.

"My name," Tal said patiently. "Here, I'll say it slower." He repeated the sound, drawing out the gutturals. It still made no sense to Holdoway. "It's th' one I answered to when I was growin' up."

Holdoway wasn't giving up. "How do you spell it?"

"I don't," Tal replied immediately. "We didn't do readin' an' writin' so good where I grew up. I had a pictogram for my name. We all had one." His calloused finger traced a pattern on the table. "Used a few names in my life, but these days I go by Tal. Seems ta work."

"Pictogram?" Holdoway shook his head. "What language did you speak?" As a Special Agent, he had access to interpreters for nearly all the common ones, and a few of the more obscure ones as well.

"Didn't have a name," Tal said bluntly. "We called it Speech, if we referred to it at all. Damn sure I'm the only person you'll find who speaks it. This goin' anywhere?"

Holdoway pressed his lips together. "What first name do you use these days?"

The suspect shrugged. "Tal. Pretty sure I just told you that."

"And last name?"

"Tal."

"So your name's Tal Tal?"

"No, *Tal*. One word. First an' last in one."

Holdoway leaned in, pressing the point. "You can't just use one name. You need a surname."

Tal raised his eyebrows. "Pretty sure most every celebrity in th' last fifty years'd take issue with that. I'm Tal, an' that's how I sign my name."

"Okay, so your name's Tal." Holdoway pretended to concede the point, where in reality he'd been setting a trap.

Using his thumb, he flicked open the folder and started pushing photographs across the table. These started out as color, then became black and white, and finally went as far back as reproductions of tintypes and daguerrotypes from two centuries before.

"Nice collection," Tal observed. "Family album?"

"Not mine," Holdoway declared. "Yours, perhaps. Or maybe just your *personal* album." He pointed at each photo in turn, indicating a specific person in each. He'd been over the images a dozen times, magnified and enhanced as far as they would go, and he was absolutely convinced of his conclusion. "That's you, isn't it? There and there and there. Every single one of these pictures is you."

Tal leaned forward and picked up one of the older ones, a daguerreotype of a Confederate Army camp with the officers sitting stiffly at attention for the photographer. Most of them had been cropped out, while in the background, side on to the viewer, he could be seen bending over a horse's hoof. "Huh," he said. "Mind if I keep this one? Didn't even know it had been done."

"So, you admit it," Holdoway said, again feeling on the back foot with the lack of push-back he was getting from Tal. "Those are all of you."

"You say so," Tal said, casting his gaze over the assembled pictures. "Just gotta say though, you might wanna get a life. This sort of obsession ain't healthy. I seen shit like this go badly wrong on folks."

Holdoway slapped his hand on the table with a loud *crack*. Tal didn't startle. "It's *you*," Holdoway insisted. "You're in all those pictures. You're that old. Don't try to deny it."

Tal leaned back in the chair. "Ain't gonna. Even if I did, you wouldn't believe me, so why bother?" He stretched, arms over head, fingers interlaced. "Bein' that old ain't a crime, so I'm still waitin' for the reason you got me sittin' in this chair, lookin' at old photos."

Regaining control of himself, Holdoway leaned forward. "You're at least two hundred and fifty years old. Do you deny it?"

There was a snort of amusement from the old man. "Damn sight older'n that, sonny boy. Still waitin' on your point."

"My *point* is that if you're so old, if you've got the grasp on history that the rest of us simply can't attain because we die inside a century, why haven't you *fixed* things?" demanded Holdoway. "All the years you've lived, all the people, cultures and inventions that have long since passed, do you remember them? Have you made any attempt at all to preserve them? Or do you even care anymore?"

Tal leaned his head back, a smile creasing new lines into his face. "Ahh," he said in tones of enlightenment. "I git it now. You ain't envious of me livin' so long … well, mebbe a little. But you're thinkin' I got a choice ta fix shit." He laughed then, the sound harshly bitter in the interview room. "Old as I am, I'm just one person. I can try an' stop things goin' ta shit right where I am, but if I try an' git more people ta listen ta me, that draws attention my way."

"And that's a *good* thing!" insisted Holdoway. "You clearly know more about how the world works than about ninety-nine percent of politicians."

"*And* a hunnerd percent of Feds, apparently," Tal countered. He leaned forward. "Lemme ask you a question, Federal boy. Suppose you're absolutely *anyone* in power, anyplace or any time, an' some asshole comes outta nowhere an' says they know where you're goin' wrong an' how ta fix it. You don't know this guy from Adam, so you tell him ta fuck off. So then he says no, wait, I'm immortal, I've seen this shit go down before, back a couple millennia ago. Do you listen to him, or do you have your flunkies grab him an' try ta figure out what makes him immortal so *you* can be immortal too?"

Holdoway opened his mouth to answer before Tal had finished, then closed it again as he registered the last few words. He raised his finger, then lowered it once more. The rational side of his brain kicked into high gear and pushed past his wishful thinking to return a result he didn't like but he knew was genuine.

"… shit," he muttered.

"Yup," agreed Tal. "Hadda run for my life once or twice. Fortunately, most everybody don't see nothing unusual about me. Just folks like you."

"Ah." Holdoway tilted his head. "So, *is* it possible—"

"Nope. The tech ain't here yet."

"I was talking about your immortality."

"So was I."

Holdoway stared at him. "How can future tech make you immortal in the past? Are you a time traveler or something?"

Tal's visage gave him nothing. "Or something." The man could indeed do a good poker face.

"Suppose I choose not to believe you on that?" Maybe a threat would make him give something up.

"Can't force you to believe shit." Or maybe it wouldn't.

"You know, if you're in Federal holding, I could make it so you spend a long, long time in a small cell. There's enough inconsistencies in your background that I could probably pull it off." He didn't like pulling out the big guns, but they existed for a reason.

That got him a derisory snort. "Sonny boy, you don't *know* from long. Now, there's one question you asked me back before, you gimme one phone call an' I'll answer it."

"Which question was that?"

Tal shook his head slowly. "Try again. Phone call, *then* answer."

The old man clearly wasn't going to give up easily. Holdoway pulled his phone out and unlocked it, then slid it across the table. Tal handled it gingerly, but he managed to tap the number in after three tries. Holding it to his ear, he waited.

"Yeah, hey, it's me. Yup yup, it's me. Long time no see, junior."

Who the hell is he calling? One of his kids? Holdoway resolved to check the number and back-trace it, once the call was done.

"Yeah, so I got this asshole called Holdoway questionin' me in the Federal building. It was fun at first, but I'm bored now. Think you can fix things?"

Holdoway's eyes opened wide and he lunged for the phone. Tal leaned back, just out of his way.

"Give me that!" shouted the Federal agent. "Give it to me now!"

"Yeah, yeah, he wants to talk to you. Sure thing. I'll be 'round later." Tal took the phone away from his ear and handed it over. "It's for you."

Holdoway snatched it away from him. "Who is this?" he demanded.

The voice he heard then was familiar to him from speeches, and once at a public appearance. *This is President Langley. I presume I'm speaking to Holdoway?*

"Uh, yes, ma'am. Special Agent Norman Holdoway, at your service." At the back of his brain, he gibbered, *How did Tal get this number?*

"You are holding a man called Tal, am I correct?" The President's tone was … chilly. At best.

"Uh, yes … he's a potential national security risk—"

The President cut him off. *"Has he been charged?"*

"Uh, no—"

"Is there evidence of a Federal crime?"

"Uh, no—"

"Then you will release him. At once. Is my meaning absolutely clear?"

"Uh, yes, ma'am."

"Good." The call ended.

Slowly, Holdoway lowered the phone to the table, and stared. "How…?" he croaked out.

Tal shrugged. "Ya live long enough, ya git contacts just about everywhere. So, I'm free ta go?"

Holdoway nodded, convulsively. "Uh, yes."

"Not gonna harass me over this bullshit again?" Tal tilted his head toward the folder.

"Uh, no."

A tight smile appeared on the old man's face. "Good. Welp, a deal's a deal. You wanted ta know how old I was, yeah?" He stood up and headed for the door.

For some reason, the words *Ya live long enough, ya git contacts just about everywhere* replayed themselves in Holdoway's head. "Yes. I would like to know that, please." After the recent conversation with his Commander in Chief, politeness seemed appropriate.

Tal opened the door, then looked back. "If I had a first name, which I don't … it'd be Neander." Stepping through, he let it close behind him.

Norman Holdoway stood in the interview room, staring at the blank wall. *Neander Tal. Neandertal.*

Oh, mother of God.

He's older than fucking humanity.

The fire was a good bit lower by the time Tal finished relating the tale. He pulled the furs around him a little tighter against the chill night air. "So I went on my way, an' never got bothered by those idiots again … well, not so's you'd notice," he wound it up.

"So, he just … didn't know who you were?" asked the boy who'd spoken up before. "But he wanted to make trouble for you because you were so old?"

Tal shrugged, moving the furs. "That's about th' long an' th' short of it, yeah."

Darnoth, Bran's father, raised his chin. "But couldn't you have advised them, as you have us? The books you have dictated, the ways to live that don't cause problems between Villages, all the secrets you have learned and passed on to us … surely they could've used them as well?"

"Oh, sure, they could have," agreed Tal. "But ya wanna teach someone somethin', ya gotta git their attention first. *You* pay attention. *They* wouldn't have, not in numbers big enough ta matter. 'Cause they thought they knew better."

"They were *silly*," said one of the younger children, and everyone laughed.

"Ain't arguin," Tal agreed. "Anyways, it's gittin' close ta my bedtime an' yours. See ya all in th' mornin'." But as the group began to break up, the children joining their parents or heading off with assurance toward their homes, Tal didn't move.

As the last of them left, Darnoth came over to where Tal sat. Subtly, he let the old, old man grasp his hand and hoist himself to his feet. "Come this way, Uncle," he said quietly. "The ground is smoother."

"Don't need your help," Tal grumbled. "Been doin' this longer'n anyone else." But he let the younger man guide him, all the same.

It was a short trek to Tal's little cottage, built of wood and native stone, and comfortably warm with a fire banked low in the hearth. Tal made it inside and settled onto his bed with a sigh of comfort. "Think I mighta pulled somethin', th' other day," he confided to Darnoth. "Ain't as young as I used to be, an' that's a fact."

"None of us are, Uncle," Darnoth agreed with a chuckle. "I'll be around in the morning."

He let himself out and closed the cottage door gently behind him. For a moment, he stood looking up at the starry night, wondering what the constellations had looked like when Tal was his age. Vastly different, from what he understood.

Before he emerged from his sleep, we were children playing at being adults, he mused. *But he taught us so much. Gave us culture and a history. Something to build on. Allowed us to create our own identity.*

We owe him everything, and we will cherish every day we spend with him.

Silently, he trod off through the trees toward his own home; a new Neandertal on an ancient world.

Chapter Twenty
Closure

Six Billion (and change) AD
Earth Rebuilt, Year 47 Post Awakening

"Don't ever get old, boy. Ain't worth th' admission ticket."

Bran smiled, the power of his muscular frame—for all that he was still a few years shy of his manhood ceremony—serving to easily move the wheeled chair over the bumpy ground toward the communal firepit. "I'll try not to, Uncle Tal."

Winter was coming once more over the Nine Villages, and the dew was beginning to turn to frost. Each and every home had been built with the chill of winter and the heat of summer in mind. The original buildings placed down by the Traveling Collective had achieved this with high-tech insulation, which had worked well enough. But when the Villages had been reconstructed to be a better fit with nature, Uncle Tal had designed the new houses with insulation derived from their very construction.

Still, the inhabitants of the Nine Villages were a communal people in their core. Even when the nights grew colder, they gathered around the firepit and roasted small snacks in the flames while Uncle Tal told tales of a land mythical to them: long ago and far away. As a small child, Bran had been enthralled by every word, trying to imagine the places and times that Tal spoke of. Now, he listened just as intently but more to the messages contained within the stories than the exploits themselves.

As for Tal himself, while he may have seemed old as time itself when he first awoke from his billion-year stasis, it seemed that his age was truly beginning to catch up with him. Just three weeks previously, he had stumbled and fallen on a smooth section of the path between two of the Villages. When he tried to get up, he fell again.

Bran's father had been walking with him at the time, and he'd immediately summoned help. Uncle Tal's lessons had passed on many skills both useful and esoteric, and willing hands immediately constructed a makeshift stretcher. Despite Tal's angry claims that he'd just tripped over a rock or something—interspersed with the most inventive swearing Bran had heard *ever*—he'd been conveyed forthwith to Riella, the primary healer for the Nine Villages.

At Tal's insistence, all members of the Nine Villages learned the modern ways of doing things, as well as the older techniques he had passed on to them since his Awakening. This meant that Riella was a fully qualified medical practitioner, even if she quite often made use of natural remedies rather than artificially produced medicines. She had examined Tal and ascertained that no bones had been broken, but all indications were that he'd suffered a minor stroke. As such, he would recover but would need to be assisted to and from the fireside gatherings they'd been holding every few days.

Tal had maintained that he was fine and could walk it off, but even a few steps with his cane left him unsteady and shaking, so Darnoth had asserted himself and told Tal that there was a solution whether he liked it or not. After all, a storyteller gathering wasn't truly worth it without the Nine Villages' best storyteller present, was it? Tal had been dubious, but Darnoth had gone away and returned two days later with a comfortable wooden chair, replete with furs and featuring a spoked wheel on each side.

Initially, Tal had raised a fuss over what he saw as a sign of weakness, and refused to even consider the concept. Fortunately, Riella had backed up Darnoth with the sweetly subtle suggestion that they could build a litter and carry Tal everywhere instead, if he'd prefer that. His roar of outrage had almost lifted the roof off the cottage, but he'd eventually settled down long enough to try out the chair. Even though he had reluctantly pronounced it comfortable enough, he hadn't been overly pleased with his forced invalid status and made sure to get out of the chair at every opportunity to prove that he could still walk.

To Riella's satisfaction, he was improving, though he still couldn't walk far; certainly not from his house to the communal firepit, or from one Village to another. That was fine, though. Such was the regard he was held in that he never lacked for a volunteer to help him get from one place to another. Today, this was Bran.

The chair bumped over the last obstacle and Bran saw the firepit up ahead, already stacked with the night's wood. Members of the Nine Villages were filtering in from all around, waving to one another and coming over to greet Tal. For his part, he sat in the chair as if the whole thing had been his idea from the very beginning. To the west, the sun was nudging the horizon, painting the clouds overhead in in vivid shades of red and gold.

"Take a good hard look at that, boy," Uncle Tal noted, indicating the sunset with a tilt of his head. "You've grown up with that sort of thing all your life, but it's a thing you surely miss when you can't see it no more."

"It *is* pretty," agreed Bran. He wondered once again at the many places Uncle Tal had lived, if he would find the Nine Villages boring by comparison. "Have you seen prettier places?"

Tal snorted and turned his head; Bran felt as though his very thoughts were being examined. "Sure. But not a one of them was home. This here's home. Ya always appreciate a place ya helped build with your own two hands."

Relieved, Bran nodded. "Is the, uh, sun different to the other one? The one you were used to?"

Turning back to the sunset, Tal frowned, the creases deepening on his face until his eyes nearly disappeared into them. "Y'know, I can't rightly tell. Th' Collective said it's a main-sequence G-type star, which was what Earth's original one was like. If there's a difference, I ain't seen it yet."

"Oh." Bran looked up at the sun again. He didn't know if it was Tal's words or something else, but for the first time he began to see it for itself, not as the same sun he'd woken up to all his life. The sunset truly *was* beautiful.

Slowly, he began to push Uncle Tal forward again, looking around occasionally to take in the sunset again. When he got to the old man's favored spot by the firepit, he let the chair roll into the ruts that had been scuffed out of the hard dirt, then took a seat beside the old man on a smoothed-down log.

Uncle Tal looked at him shrewdly and put a calloused hand on his arm. "Thanks, kid. Ya don't need ta stick around. I'll be fine if ya got somethin' you'd rather be doin'." He nodded significantly toward a bunch of girls around Bran's age who had just come into view. A few of them looked over and waved.

Bran waved back, then lowered his voice. "Thanks, Uncle Tal. But there was something I wanted to ask you. I, um, Stefan has offered me a place in the Academy. He says I've got the aptitude to go into space. You've always said our place is right here on Earth, but I feel like I could really do it. Father says I should ask you. What should I do?"

"Whoa, whoa, kid." Tal shook his head. "You got me wrong. I've always said *my* place is right here on Earth. You figure you wanna travel, leave th' Nine Villages an' go out there, be my guest. My destiny ain't your destiny. Never was, never will be. Okay?"

The import of Uncle Tal's words left Bran staggering, mentally if not physically. "Uh … I … wow … yes … okay. Okay!" He felt light-headed at the rush of relief through his system. "Thanks, Uncle Tal. That means a lot."

"Eh, ain't nothin'." Tal chuckled. "Learned a long, long time ago, th' best way ta make sure someone does somethin' is ta tell 'em they can't. Say they can, at least they stop an' think about it an' don't jump in feet first."

Bran nodded at the implicit message. "I'll be careful. I promise."

"An' that's all we c'n ask for." Tal lowered his brows and gave him a serious look. "Just remember. Sometimes you c'n take all th' care in th' world an' shit will still happen. Don't assume it won't, just 'cause ya crossed all th' Ts an' all that. Always have a plan ta git th' hell outta Dodge, just in case. *Always.*"

"Get out of ... Dodge?" Bran tilted his head.

Tal chuckled. "A place that was, long time ago. Went there once. Never had ta leave in a hurry, but some places I did. Just never assume that shit can't go sideways. 'Cause it absolutely can."

"I understand." Bran stood up and squeezed Uncle Tal's shoulder. "And thanks. I appreciate it."

"Ain't nothin', boy." He made a dismissive gesture. "Now, git. Go have fun."

"I will, and thank you again." Bran left the old man's side and headed off, the tough grass springy under his feet. He spotted where the girls were chatting with some boys he knew, and moved in that direction. *I'm going to the Academy!* he exulted.

But tonight, as Uncle Tal had intimated, was for fun.

Night had fallen, and a sharp breeze was blowing across the hillside. Uncle Tal pulled the furs a little closer around himself, recalling when such a thing wouldn't have bothered him in the slightest. *There you are, Mr Tal! You can't be standing out here! You'll catch a chill!*

He'd looked old then as he did now, but inside he was starting to catch up. He'd been in the Nine Villages for forty-seven years now, each year of which he'd lived to its full. Teaching, telling stories, dictating books, awakening a culture within his people. But time had taken its toll. Year by year, his body became less capable of overcoming such things, leading toward the inevitable end. He wasn't looking forward to it, exactly, but he'd long ago accepted it.

Three of the men were bent over the firepit, busy with fire-starters. One tiny flame began, only to be snuffed out by a vagrant breeze. Another one licked upward, then caught. The wind fanned it; instead of flickering to its demise, it strengthened. Gradually, the fire spread throughout the stacked wood, and there was a muted cheer from the gathered crowd.

For awhile, there was chatter between everyone there. Tal spoke with Darnoth, who had taken Bran's seat, about the boy's chances of graduating from the Academy. People brought food and hot drinks, while others toasted foodstuffs over the flames. But then, as the conversations died down, more and more people turned toward Tal.

"Tell us a story, Uncle Tal," one of the children said, opening the years-long ritual.

"Yes, Uncle Tal," another one chimed in. "Tell us a story."

Tal chuckled. "I got one for ya," he said, pitching his voice so that all could hear. It helped that the only other sounds were the crackling of the flames and the keening of the wind through the grass. "You all remember the Egyptian lady, Khemet, an' how she was Sleeping years at a time?"

A chorus of agreement came back to him. That had been one of his more popular stories, but for some reason he'd never told anyone how that tale had ended.

"So, a couple hunnerd years later, just about the beginning of th' twenty-third century, I managed ta be there when she Woke up. An' I had some good news for her."

2202 AD
Southern California

"You know, for the longest time I thought I was the only one," mused Khemet, leaning with her elbows on the boardwalk railing. The sun had just set over the ocean, but the lingering rays were still in the sky. "The only immortal, I mean." The language she spoke was one that had not been in common use for thousands of years, and yet she was fluent in it.

"Yeah, I know how that goes," agreed her companion, speaking the same tongue but with a less refined accent. "It's not like it's an easy thing ta make happen. Time machines got safety measures, so it's gotta be a total screw-up or somethin' deliberate. I only know about one other guy myself."

"Really?" she turned to stare at him. "Who is he? *Where* is he?"

"Sorry." He shook his head. "By now he's already wrapped around to where he started off from. Th' plan was that once his younger self left, he was just gonna step in an' take over his life again. Dunno where he is, an' I don't wanna. He's th' dick that did this ta me in th' first place."

"Oh." Khemet decided she wanted to hear that story at some point, but she didn't want to press him on it right now when she had more important things to worry about. "So, uh, have you managed to make any progress on my situation?"

Tal's teeth gleamed white in the fading light. "Yup. Had a good look through th' time traveler register. Found this one guy who's had his licence pulled a couple times for dodgy stuff, but they could never make it stick. Fits th' description of th' asshole as did this ta you. Wanna know th' funny thing, though?"

She could never be sure what he considered 'funny' or just plain weird, but she was willing to find out. "Sure."

"I've met that sonovabitch before." He snorted in amusement. "For a while there, every time I recognized a time traveler for what they were,

I'd beat the snot out of them an' kick 'em back to their own time. First few times you woke up, I was in th' area. Didn't know about you an' him, of course, but when I twigged what he was, I tuned him up some an' sent him home. This happened two, three more times over th' next couple centuries. Now, what *he* was doin' was tryin' ta pick up your trail again so's he could have his way with you. But by th' time I moved on, you were outta th' area. Figure he's still tryin' ta track ya down."

"Oh, *really?*" Now that she knew the 'grand mage' who had done this to her was nothing more than an opportunistic time traveler, she'd gone from being fatalistic about her situation to being angry. "So, what do you think I should do? Have him arrested? Will it even matter?" She wasn't sure if time travelers could even *be* charged for crimes committed in a different era, when their actions were no longer seen as criminal.

He waggled his hand from side to side. "Technically, yeah, it'll matter. Realistically, all he has ta do is drag it out for a month, until th' victim an' th' star witness isn't able ta testify anymore. Figure he'd get a suspended sentence at best."

"So he wins." She was unable to keep the bitterness from her voice. "We know who he is and what he's done, but we can't do anything about it."

To her surprise, he chuckled, deep and long. "Oh, I didn't say *that.*"

The building was silent, except for the almost inaudible cycling of the air conditioning, and the subliminal crackling of electricity. The museum was still operational, though fewer and fewer people were interested in viewing relics of the past when time travel meant that one could *go* there.

On the other hand, time seemed to operate via a modified version of the Observer Principle; specifically, whatever state of affairs that existed in the present before the traveler went back would still be there when they returned. Hitler (and his grandfather) were effectively safe from temporal shenanigans, because World War Two *had* happened, and would *always* have happened.

This meant that, in spite of all the efforts to the contrary, time travelers could not go back and snatch some historical treasure when it was being guarded laxly or not at all, thus depriving the museum of its use. Something *always* happened to prevent such, because *it had not happened.* Even those who arranged for near-identical replicas with which to replace the item rarely succeeded, except in the cases of those institutions that failed to check over their acquisitions with a fine-tooth comb before displaying them.

Of course, this only served to dissuade those who lacked imagination. Case in point: one Gaspar Fenley, jewel thief and all-round dirtbag. Fenley was an amateur Egyptologist who had made several trips to the era in question, with the aim of making himself rich by selling off items back when they were much more valuable. Unfortunately for him, the rules of time travel had prevented him from grabbing anything too noteworthy, though he'd used his stasis gun on a few of them anyway.

He was very proud of the stasis gun. Making use of a totally illegal modification to his chronon storage banks, the gun dosed whatever it was fired at with chronons, effectively slowing it down and putting it into a state where it could not be harmed by anything. Sometimes this protection flickered, but that was a problem he couldn't be bothered fixing.

So he'd tried another tack. Going back, he created the persona of a great and powerful mage. So far, this was fine. If the rules worked the way people said — and he hadn't seen anything to the contrary — nothing he did or said would reach his home time as the work of a time traveler. It would just be another wild story. But while he was there, he could *earn* (not steal) whatever they were willing to pay him to demonstrate his 'magic'. He was sure museums in his present would be willing to pay top dollar for unspoiled coinage of the era.

The plan was going fine, right up until he saw *her*. The daughter of one of the noblemen who frequented the palace, perhaps sixteen years old. A beautiful face and equally pleasant nature. Enquiring, he found that Khemet (for such was her name) was not betrothed to anyone yet (which, to be honest, wouldn't truly have bothered him) but her father would not be averse to an alliance with such a powerful worker of the mystic arts.

Thus emboldened, he presented himself to her, stating that he had chosen her as his consort, and that she would be his bride before the month was out (he only planned to stay a little longer, anyway). He was rich, he reminded her. He was powerful. She would be showered with all the luxuries she could want.

Thank you, she said with a kindly smile, but no.

Fenley was astonished and enraged. He was a *time traveler,* a veritable *god* to these primitive savages. How *dare* she reject him! She should be *begging* him for his time, rather than turning away to tend to her garden.

What had been a passing fancy turned into an obsession. He could not be seen to assault her where her family would find out, for that way led to an ugly death beneath bronze blades. But he could be tricky about it. He had himself invited to her father's house, and by careful questioning learned the location of her bedroom. Then he excused himself, jumped forward to a point when the house was abandoned, then went to that same bedroom. Jumping back, he found himself in her room as she was just dressing for the day.

She was startled and upset by his presence, which wasn't helped when he pressed his case once more. She told him no, much more vehemently. He grabbed her by the arm; she snatched up a small but sharp dagger and stabbed him (not deeply, but it hurt like hell). Enraged, he shoved her away from him and pulled the stasis gun. The pulse enveloped her, but she didn't freeze immediately. Instead, she seemed to become extremely tired and lay down upon the bed.

At that moment, he heard servants pounding on the door and calling out, so he time-jumped out of there, back to his home time; wounds suffered in the past were never to be taken lightly. The chances of infection or even disease getting in were all too high.

When he returned to that location, a few years later in local time, he found that the lady Khemet had been found in her bedchamber in a state of mystical mummification, and that she had been interred in the family crypt. He decided to go directly to when the stasis was due to wear off (at least temporarily), about sixty years in the future. Perhaps then she would be more amenable to his advances.

Unfortunately, when he got there, he encountered a brutish figure of foreign extraction, who seemed to take violent exception to him for no reason he could understand. After a vicious beating, he left that time, never to return. He would instead go to the next time that she was due to emerge from stasis, leaving the brutish stranger in the past.

That didn't happen. Once again, he encountered someone who was either that very same person or their direct descendant. Either way, they disliked him for some unknown reason, and once more attacked him with little in the way of provocation. He was left to travel onward in time, bruised and battered and wondering what the hell was going on.

Four more times he attempted to catch up with Khemet, but twice his timing was out and twice he encountered that brutal stranger yet again. When Fenley tried to call on him as a fellow time traveler, he denied it — in English! — and delivered the most brutal trouncing yet.

Fenley knew when he was beaten. The universe didn't want him catching up with her. So he would have to wait until she showed up in his present day. He kept an eye out for any newsfeeds that might show her face, while he got treatment for his broken bones.

And then he saw it; or rather, an aggressive advertising campaign jumped out at him. A dinky little museum in Los Angeles of all places, with a display that included a sleeping Khemet as the centerpiece. A few years older now, she looked to be about twenty-one, but she was still as captivating as ever. And if his calculations were correct, she was due to emerge from stasis in a day or so.

It was time to utilize the same trick as he had in the nobleman's house back in ancient Egypt. Traveling to Los Angeles, he visited the museum and joined a tour group, *ooh*-ing and *aah*-ing at the various displays. When he got the chance, he ducked away to the restrooms and jumped forward twelve hours.

Picking his way through the darkened building, avoiding the motion sensors he'd already noted down, past a life-sized model of a Neandertal in the hallway, he found his way finally in the Ancient Egypt display. Drawing the stasis gun, he edged toward it. This close to coming out of stasis, Khemet's body could have the chronons drawn out of it so that he could wake her up. This time, he decided coldly, she would be his whether she wanted to be or not.

And there she lay, on her bier, arms crossed over her body, still and silent. He moved up beside her, admiring the slim lines of her body. She had grown even more beautiful in the intervening—for her—six years. Well, she was all his now. He began to raise the stasis gun, then noticed something odd.

Under her crossed hands, her chest rose slightly.

She was waking up *now.*

Jamming the pistol back into its holster, he reached for her arm … and that was when something tapped him on the shoulder. Profoundly startled, he spun around, only to come face to face with the Neandertal model.

What's that thing doing in here?

Oh. It's not a model.

He never saw the punch that knocked him cold.

Tal filled a bucket of water from the sink and splashed it over the bound man's face. "Wakey wakey, asshole."

Fenley spluttered and gasped and struggled back to consciousness, looking around dazedly. He saw Tal first, holding the bucket. Then he saw Khemet, wearing a T-shirt and blue jeans—and absolutely rocking it, in Tal's personal opinion—perching on one of the benches in the restroom.

"Wh-what?" he managed. "What's going on?" Then he clearly realized that his hands were tied behind him, tried briefly to free himself, then gave up. "Let me go! What is this?"

"*This* is you reversing whatever it was you did to me," Khemet said, sliding forward off the bench. "You've been stalking me for five thousand years. It ends, tonight. Now. Or …" She indicated Tal with a sideways tilt of her head. The implication was clear.

Fenley certainly thought so, because he tried again to get out of his bonds. Tal had learned to tie knots from experts in the field, so he knew the guy wasn't going anywhere. "You!" Fenley gasped, looking at Tal.

"What's your stake in this? Why are you helping her? What's she paying you?"

"Paying?" Tal snorted. "Nothing. I just hate time travelers, is all." He picked up the stasis gun. "How's this thing work?" Experimentally, he sighted in on Fenley's prone form.

"D-don't!" squawked the thief. "It infuses the target with chronons! I'd freeze, and you'd never get anything more out of me!"

"Hm." Tal nodded in Khemet's direction. "You used it on her. How come she's awake?"

"It's a glitch in the delivery mechanism," babbled Fenley. "Every sixty years or so, living things come out of stasis for a little while."

"Right." Tal loomed in menacingly. "So, how do I reverse it?"

"And that deals with that." Khemet let Tal out through the loading-dock door, reset the alarm and joined him outside the building.

"Damn right." Under one arm, Tal carried the time traveler's temporal rig. Under the other, there was a small cabinet with a closely fitting door. "Think th' museum's gonna kick up a stink over you bein' gone, or stolen, or whatever?"

She let out a light chuckle. "I really don't care. I never got paid. My deal was with William, and he's a hundred years dead. They're just going to have to live with having a statue of a high mage from the Lower Kingdom. He's even mentioned a couple of times in the historical record." She nodded at the time-travel gear. "What are you going to do with that?"

With a grunt, Tal put down the temporal gear, then with rather more care, he placed the cabinet on the ground. "The guy I knew told me about these things," he said, turning the temporal rig over. "They all come with one specific safety feature: a go-home button. If ya find yourself in the middle of some battle and an asshole comes runnin' at you with a big-ass axe, ya don't wanna spend time calculatin' your next jump." He flipped up a cover to reveal a red button, recessed into the casing. "Hit this an' you go straight back to where you bought it."

"Which has a record of whoever bought it." Khemet indicated the stasis gun and a few other things that were clearly after-market modifications. "And do you think they'll be pleased to see those?"

Tal grinned. "Not even a little bit." Finding a stick nearby, he prodded the button cautiously with it. The temporal rig flickered once, then vanished. So did half the stick.

As he hefted the cabinet once more, he nodded at it. "So, what are you gonna do with all this? I mean, you're not gonna keep writing up the record, are ya?"

"No, I don't think so." She tilted her head. "But this is something I've worked on for years. I don't want to just leave it behind. Maybe I'll write a book or something. Once I figure out where I'm living and what I'm doing. Got any suggestions?"

"A few." He shifted the weight of the cabinet. "Few hunnerd years ago, you asked about the chance of gittin' a trust fund. I c'n still make that happen. Got th' contacts ta have ya granted citizenship, easy. You c'n settle down anywhere ya like, write your book, live your life. Whaddaya say?"

Khemet stepped up alongside Tal and put her arm around his shoulders. When she spoke, her voice indicated tears unshed. "I say … thank you."

"And what happened *then*, Uncle Tal?" asked one of the younger children. "Did she live happily ever after?"

Tal chuckled warmly. "She surely did. Lived a long an' full life, wrote a shelf full o' books. I even read some of 'em."

He stretched, arching his back to work the kinks out of his spine. The furs slipped off his shoulders just as a vicious swirl of wind came through, blowing smoke everywhere. Caught by surprise, he broke into a fit of coughing. It felt like something was trying to scrape out the bottom of his lungs with a jagged piece of flint. Pulling the furs back around his chest, he tried to catch his breath, but the coughing just got worse.

Eventually, with Darnoth patting him on the back, he got the better of it, and the spasms eased. He sipped at a hot drink someone passed him, and felt his breathing improve. There was still a tingling sensation when he tried to inhale too deeply, but he figured that would pass.

"Are you alright, Uncle Tal?" asked Bran. "Do you want me to take you back home?"

Tal waved him away impatiently. "I'm fine. A bit of smoke in the face, is all. I had worse, never got hot an' bothered about it." He took a deeper drink from the rich brew in the cup he was holding. "So, who wants ta hear about th' time I ended up in th' Roman army?"

A dozen hands went up. "Me!" shouted the children. "Me! Me! Me!"

Tal finished the cup and handed it off to Darnoth. "Okay, then. There I was, in a tavern with this feller I knew called Lucio, mindin' my own business, an' in comes this *optio* with a couple of legionaries followin' along. He starts talkin' up big about all th' benefits of signin' up with th' military right now. I wasn't totally sold on it, but Lucio was tryin' ta impress a girl, so he signed up. So I did too, ta keep an eye on him. Well anyways, we marched off toward Gaul …"

Chapter Twenty-One
The Last Story

Six Billion (and change) AD
Earth Rebuilt, Year 47 Post Awakening

Uncle Tal was uncharacteristically quiet on the way back to his house, after the gathering around the firepit had broken up. Bran knew the way; he'd been over this ground nearly every day of his life. The farthest he'd been away from the Nine Villages was to visit the fishing villages on the coast a few miles to the north, but if he went away to the Academy, he'd be leaving everything he ever knew behind.

"Uncle Tal?" he asked quietly, as they approached the house.

There was silence for a moment, and Bran wondered if the old man had fallen asleep, but then he stirred. "Yeah?" asked Tal, but the word was interrupted by a cough. He cleared his throat and tried again. "Yeah, what is it?"

"Is it hard?" asked Bran. "Going off to someplace new, knowing you might never see your home again?"

Silence passed between them for a moment, then Tal nodded in the dimness. "Surely is. Harder ta leave it when everyone you know's still alive an' kickin', but it ain't never easy ta move on." He paused to cough, then went on. "You should find it easier'n I did, though. Figure Stefan'll be able ta arrange it so's your family c'n send you messages. When I moved on, I never did know what I'd find if I ever got back there. Or if there'd *be* a 'there' when I got back. You come home on leave, th' Nine Villages'll be right here waitin'. Mebbe a little bigger, mebbe a little different, but it'll still be here."

He broke off into a coughing fit, hunching forward in his furs. Bran waited, feeling awkward, patting him lightly on the back. While the whole tribe had been given training in basic first aid—another thing Uncle Tal had insisted on—he didn't know what to do in this situation.

Eventually, Uncle Tal straightened up again. "Goddamn it," he rasped, wiping the back of his hand across his mouth. "Git me inside, boy. I need ta warm these old bones up."

"Yes, Uncle Tal." Bran opened the door and wheeled the chair into the house. The fire banked in the hearth had kept the interior considerably warmer than the chill wind outside, and Bran immediately felt himself starting to sweat inside his own furs.

Once in the warm, Uncle Tal climbed out of the chair and made his way into the bedroom. "You git on home now, boy," he called out. "An' good luck with th' Academy!"

"I will, and thank you." Bran parked the chair neatly at the side of the room, and went to the front door. As he stepped out and closed it behind him, he heard Uncle Tal starting to cough again. With a frown, he pulled the door all the way closed and started along a pathway away from his parents' house.

Riella came awake to a thumping at her front door. She checked the simple mechanical alarm clock that sat next to the window, and grimaced. According to the time it displayed, she'd only gotten to bed a couple of hours ago. But just as the members of the Nine Villages knew not to bother her unnecessarily for her healing expertise, she knew that they wouldn't be calling on her if there wasn't a problem.

Still, she muttered a few unkind words as she climbed out of bed and threw on a wrap before heading to the front door. Opening it, she gasped slightly at the knife-edged chill of the air, then focused on her visitor. "Bran," she said. "Come on in."

"Thank you." He accepted her invitation, shivering slightly despite his furs.

She closed the door and looked him up and down. He didn't appear to be injured, so the problem was elsewhere. "Who is it?" she asked.

"Uncle Tal," he said quietly. "I think he may be ill. He started coughing at the gathering, and he was still coughing when I got him home where it was warm."

Her eyes opened wide and she forgot all about her lost sleep. "That stubborn, cantankerous old fool!" she snapped. "I've told him and told him to wrap up properly! How bad was it?"

"Pretty bad," he admitted. "That's why I came straight here."

"Right. Thank you. You've done exactly the right thing." She slapped him on the shoulder, but she was already going over in her head what she was going to need. "Now I'm going to need you to do something for me."

Young he may have been, but he straightened up and threw back his shoulders. "What do you need?" he asked, as if uncaring that the blade-sharp wind outside would slice straight through his clothing.

Well, the boy came from good stock. Darnoth was as tough as they came, and all Neandertal in the Nine Villages were effectively descended from Uncle Tal himself, so she figured he could take a little more punishment in a good cause. "Go to Stefan. Tell him I need antibiotics, and fast."

"Antibiotics," he repeated. "Do I tell him they're for Uncle Tal?"

"Only if he asks," she said firmly. "We don't want to spread unnecessary worry. It might well be something we can deal with easily."

Or it might not, which was why she wasn't waiting until morning.

He nodded once, sharply; a habit copied from his father. "On my way." Wrapping his jacket more closely around himself, he turned and opened the door, allowing a chill wind to sweep through the house. Without even a word of complaint, he stepped outside and vanished into the night, just as a scud of snow swept past.

Snow or no snow, Uncle Tal needed her help. Riella shut the door and rapidly began to pack her medical bag with everything she figured she'd need. Her supply of antibiotics was low, because there was little need for it. Barely anyone in the Nine Villages got sick, and those who did recovered quickly, mainly due to their solid genetic heritage.

Also, because Uncle Tal had insisted that the Traveling Collective isolate every single disease agent—bacterial and viral—running around in his bloodstream, and vaccinate the Nine Villages against them. It had been an impressive collection.

With the bag full, she shrugged into her full-length winter fur jacket and heavy boots—bare feet were well and good for daytime, but not so much when frostbite was a near-certainty—and made her way out into the burgeoning snowstorm.

It was an unpleasant journey to Tal's cottage, but she never lost her way or worried about getting there. Driving snow collected on her upwind side, and the chill bit straight through the fur to nip at her skin. She set her jaw and kept going; a little discomfort wasn't going to stop her doing what she had to.

Still and all, when she got there, she let out a huff of relief. There was no light in the window, but that only meant he didn't have a lamp lit. Her eyes were well-adjusted to the dark, and she knew the layout of his home, so she wouldn't have a problem. *Except maybe with the cranky old idiot himself.*

As she raised her hand to knock, there was a lull in the wind and she heard the coughing from within. It was only a brief interlude, but it decided her. She knocked and opened the door more or less at the same moment; the wind was doing its best to flay the flesh from her bones.

"Who—" Another wracking cough. "Who's there?"

"It's Riella," she called out, stamping the snow off her boots and shrugging out of the jacket. Coals still glimmered in the hearth, and warmth pervaded the small dwelling. "Bran came to me and said you were coughing. I came straight over."

"I'm fine." Another round of deep phlegmy hacking gave the lie to that statement. "Just a little chill. I'll git over it."

She took up her bag again and went through into the bedroom. Sitting hunched over in bed, he glared at her. She ignored it. "Tal, you're literally older than anyone who's ever lived."

"I was in stasis for most of it," he grumbled.

"Not for ninety thousand years and change, you weren't," she countered, opening the bag. It was an article of faith in the Nine Villages that simpler technology was better than something that would probably break down at the wrong moment, so the thermometer she pulled out was built around the ancient 'alcohol in a plastic tube' model.

"That was chronons," he managed before starting to cough again. She rubbed his back gently, trying to soothe his spasms, then put the thermometer in his mouth before he could object. To his credit, he didn't spit it out again.

"That's true," she allowed. "But you could've been anything from twenty to thirty when you were infused, so you're at least sixty, and maybe in your seventies. And we don't *know* what the average lifespan was, when you were born. You could be looking at another twenty years, or be ten years over the norm. So, I'm going to treat this as serious."

Taking her worn old alarm clock out of the bag, she captured his wrist and started counting his pulse while keeping an eye on the second hand. Once she'd gotten her result—his heart rate was elevated, which didn't surprise her—she took the thermometer out and peered at it. "Damn it, you're running a temperature already," she muttered. It was only a degree or so, but that was more than enough.

"Nothin' a good night's sleep won't fix," he muttered. "Been sick before. Got over it just fine."

"I'm not convinced your chronons didn't just keep you healthy until the infection gave up," she countered. "The number of diseases that the Collective found inside you was *insane.*" She took a deep breath. "Okay, the first thing we need to do is to loosen up that phlegm and get it out of your lungs ..."

Turning back to her bag, she replaced the thermometer in its case. Tal would complain about the medicine, but that was just his way. She was descended from his genetic material, just as everyone in the Nine Villages were, and she was damned if she was going to let him out-stubborn her in this matter.

"Down there!" Bran pointed through the swirling gusts of snow at where he knew Tal's cottage to be.

"Yup, I see it now." Stefan, handling the controls of the grav-lifter with the finesse of someone who'd been doing it for more than a century, brought the small craft in for a neat landing in the clearing next to the building.

As soon as he felt the skids jar to a halt, Bran grabbed the bag that Riella had requested and popped the canopy. "Thanks!" he called out to

Stefan and ran toward the door of the building, slowing only to take care that he didn't fall. Behind him, the lifter shut down altogether.

Crap. He's getting out. Riella's gonna find out I told him.

Well, it couldn't be helped now. He knocked briefly—it was *cold* out!—then entered. As he did so, Riella leaned around the bedroom doorway. "I brought the antibiotics," Bran said, holding up the carton Stefan had given him.

"Good," she said. "It's gotten a good hold on him, but maybe we can knock it out before it gets too far." She tilted her head as she took the carton from him. "You got back faster than I expected."

"That's because he came back with me." Stefan pushed the door open behind Bran. "I had to ask him directly before he'd give me a straight answer. How bad is it?"

She set her jaw grimly. "Too early to tell. It might pass overnight, or it might be a deeper thing. Now hush, and let me work." As she turned back toward the bedroom, she gestured at the hearth. "If you want to make yourselves useful, get some wood and build the fire up. Warmth is his best chance, right now."

Stefan looked at Bran and shrugged. "Looks like we've got our orders. Where's Tal keep his woodpile?"

Hesitating for a second as he thought it out, Bran gestured. "Out the door, around to the right. Just step wide around his vegetable patch. He gets testy if we walk in it."

"He grows vegetables?" Stefan raised his eyebrows before he pulled his hood back over his head.

"He grows whatever he likes," Bran corrected him. "A few years ago, he had flowers there." He opened the door and stepped out into the biting cold.

"Huh. Sounds about right." Stefan followed him.

In the morning, Uncle Tal was no better, but he was no worse either. Riella detailed one of her fellow healers to care for him while she went home and caught up on sleep, but she was back by the evening. It continued to snow, but the inhabitants of the Nine Villages were a hardy lot. Trodden-down paths quickly emerged, and were widened by Bran and the other youngsters wielding snow-shovels.

Over the next week, she nursed him through a particularly nasty chest infection, hammering it with large doses of antibiotics and Vitamin C, the age-old remedy. Stefan offered nano-healers that would've cleared the matter up in minutes, but Tal turned the man down flat and Riella supported his decision. It was his right, she stated, to refuse treatment he'd not agreed to. Whether he'd agreed to the treatment *she* was providing, she neglected to say.

After the seventh day, once the snow passed by and the weather warmed, his fever broke and his condition began to improve. Still, she noted that his lungs were still weak and advised him to refrain from heavy exercise until he was feeling better. He responded in his usual irritated manner, and she noted that he must be feeling better.

As spring rolled around, Uncle Tal could be seen once more, walking along the paths amidst the freshly growing flowers and aromatic grasses. Everyone had heard of his illness, and so they were glad to see him, though they made sure not to crowd him as he went upon his way. If people noticed that he leaned a little more heavily on his walking stick, or that his step was a little slower and less sure than before, nobody spoke about it. They were just pleased that he was back.

Over the course of that spring and summer, he walked farther abroad than he had since the stroke had put him in the chair. Each and every Village he visited in its turn, with Darnoth and Bran at his side. Some of these he knew well, and some he'd only seen at their Founding, but he paid equal attention to each. And as they gathered around him in each one, he told a story, and smiled as he told it. Each story, as far as Darnoth knew, was one that he'd never told before.

Still, Riella had warned him that Uncle Tal's lungs had been damaged by the illness and that he must not be allowed to suffer from the cold or the damp. So Darnoth made sure that they had lodging in every village that they came to, and that Tal had the warmest place to sleep. Day after day, they walked onward, until even Darnoth began to wonder at Tal's new burst of energy.

"Why are you doing this?" he asked one evening, back in Tal's house. "Aren't you worried you'll wear yourself out again?"

Tal snorted and gave him a side-eyed glance. "You been listenin' ta Riella too much. Ain't that I'm wearin' myself out. Way I see it, I got so many ticks of th' clock, an' it's up ta me ta decide how ta use 'em. Some o' them kids, they hadn't never heard one o' my stories, not from me anyways. So I'm goin' around an' seein' all th' Villages, while there's still time."

"Time?" That word sounded ominous, and Darnoth looked over at Tal.

"Before winter, naturally." Tal snorted. "Won't catch me walkin' in th' winter. Ain't gonna let Riella put me through *that* crap again."

"Oh. Right." They talked on, and Tal changed the subject. Eventually, Darnoth forgot that it had ever been raised.

Summer rolled toward autumn. Bran, to the cheers of the Village, went off to attend the Academy. Tal was there as the ship lifted off, leaning on his stick as always, his ancient, lined face bearing an expression of pure pride.

He kept walking, although he'd visited all the Neandertal settlements, as far and wide as they'd spread in the decades since he'd emerged into the sunlight for the first time on the Earth rebuilt. Once, with Darnoth's assistance, he struggled up the tallest hill in the area, which he declared was a prime location to watch the sunset from. To this end, twenty or thirty years previously, he'd rough-hewn a couple of log seats and enlisted the aid of the Village adults to drag them up the hill. Now, once he got up there, he was pleased to be able to fall into them and catch his breath.

Watching the sun as it spread its glory over the western sky, he half-turned toward Darnoth. "I want Bran ta have th' house."

"What?" Darnoth didn't understand at first.

"Bran. When he comes home, he gits th' house, assumin' I'm not around when he does." Tal's announcements were as blunt as ever. "He went lookin' for Riella when I was sick, an' was like ta run across th' Village an' back in a howlin' snowstorm ta git me th' medicine I needed. He gits th' house."

Darnoth nodded. "I understand." And, looking at Tal, he understood more than that.

For all his immense will, the oldest man in the village was slowly losing the battle against entropy. He was not going gentle into that good night, as a poem Tal had once disclaimed authorship of had said. His was a slow and steady fighting retreat. He had chosen the time and place of his death once before, and he would do so again, and he would spit in the face of destiny if it dared say otherwise.

They watched as the last light faded from the western sky, and then Darnoth rose and helped Tal to his feet. More and more, Tal needed this, these days, but Darnoth would have sooner allowed his tongue to be torn out by the roots than mention it to the man he walked beside. Slowly and carefully, they descended the hill, and Darnoth walked Uncle Tal back to his cottage.

Days turned into weeks, and Tal's walks around the village became shorter and shorter. And then one day they ceased altogether, when Tal said he didn't feel like it. The dark foreboding Darnoth had felt since the conversation on the hilltop returned to him, and he went directly from Tal's house to fetch Riella.

Three days later, in the middle of the afternoon, there was a tap upon Darnoth's door. He answered it, to find Riella's oldest standing there. A bright girl of about fifteen, he had often thought Mareli would be a good match for Bran. But right now, he wasn't thinking about his son.

"Can … can I help you?" he asked, needing to force out the words.

He knew what was going on, but he had to ask anyway.

"Mam says to come now," Mareli said, looking as solemn as he felt. "She says he's asking for you."

"I'm on my way." He snatched up his jacket, for the chill was settling earlier and earlier each day, then kissed his wife and dashed out the door.

Mareli was young and fleet of foot, but he passed her before they got halfway there, and left her in his dust. Pausing at the entrance to Tal's cottage to catch his breath, he tapped on the door then entered. In the cozy front room, Stefan turned to look at him, his face showing lines of stress that he hadn't had before.

"Oh, good," said the human, relief flooding his features. "You're here."

"I came as soon as Mareli fetched me." Darnoth kept his voice down out of respect. "How is he?"

"I'm dying, not deaf!" The irascible voice from the bedroom was clearly audible. "Git in here, boy."

Though Darnoth was far from being a 'boy'—he had been a respected voice in the running of the Nine Villages for years—he did not quibble over the appellation. Not when it was bestowed by Uncle Tal. The Nine Villages had their elders, but Tal was *the* Elder. Although he disliked the term, it was well-earned.

As Stefan moved aside to let him pass, Darnoth nodded a silent thanks to him. He knew that Stefan, as the local representative of the Traveling Collective, would have been pleading with Uncle Tal to allow life-extension treatments to be performed upon him, and he was just as aware of Tal's opinion of such things. And as much as they would've liked to force the issue, they had far too much respect for the old man to ignore his wishes.

Tal himself was lying back in his comfortable bed, with Riella attending to him. "I'm here," Darnoth said simply. "What do you need?"

A little to his surprise—but not overly much—it was Tal who replied, not Riella. "I need ta git outta here," he said. "Need ta see th' open sky. Watch th' sunset. Been too long since I did that."

"You will not be doing that," Riella snapped. "The chill will be coming over soon. You'll—"

"I'll *what?*" he asked scornfully. "Catch my death o' cold? Been there, done that. Tell ya what. You c'n flap your gums about what I should an' shouldn't be doin', or you c'n come along an' keep an eye on me."

Riella looked at Darnoth for assistance, but he said nothing. It was Uncle Tal's decision to do what he wanted, as it always had been. Finally, she huffed in exasperation. "You'll never get up there. You're too weak to walk that far, and Darnoth isn't going to be carrying you."

"So put me in that damn chair," Tal retorted. "You were all so pleased when he made it for me. Might as well put it to good use." He nodded toward the corner of his bedroom where the offending item had spare furs and other items piled over it. "Near on cut it up ta use for firewood once. Didn't know why I didn't. Now I do."

Darnoth looked at Riella and shrugged, raising his eyebrows. Uncle Tal had a point, and they both knew it.

"... fine," she growled, folding her arms. "But I *am* coming along, and I'm not helping push the chair."

"Wouldn't dream of askin' ya to," Tal said, swinging his legs over the side of the bed. "Now git that monstrosity over here before I change my damn mind."

Climbing the hill was normally not difficult, but pushing Tal in his chair made it slightly more challenging. It didn't help that Darnoth himself wasn't as young or athletic as he used to be, but they made it without mishap. Riella climbed alongside, keeping a critical eye on both Tal and Darnoth, but mainly on Tal.

When they reached the summit, Darnoth scuffed out ruts for the chair's wheels to rest in, between the two seats that had been set up by Tal. He was more glad than he was willing to admit that the seats were there; a leading figure in the Nine Villages, greying hair and all, had no place pushing laden chairs up hills. Although if he were challenged on the matter, he would not begrudge Uncle Tal the chance to appreciate this view one last time. Up here, the wind blew fresh and sweet, and one could see for miles in every direction.

They did not speak much, each concerned with their own thoughts, save for Tal himself. Even as he took in the view, the old man related one anecdote after another, picking and choosing apparently at random from the vast tapestry of his life. Darnoth realized after awhile that they had a similar theme; letting go, moving on, dealing with loss.

"... but yeah, eventually I was th' only resident, which kinda went against th' purpose of th' whole thing." He sighed in reminiscence. "No more protective camouflage if there ain't nobody else there. So, I closed th' doors an' moved out. Gave th' title over to th' last attendants ta live there if they wanted. Went out in th' world again. It was good while it lasted, though. Kept it goin' for nigh on a hunnerd fifty years. Closest I had to a real home for a long, long time." Gradually his voice fell away and he sank back into the furs.

"Alright, that's it," Riella stated once it was clear he wasn't about to start another story. "The day's almost done. Time to get you home. Both of you."

Tal roused himself and gave her a glare that would almost have passed muster from the days when he was working to bring the Nine Villages into being. "Nope," he stated. "I wanna stay an' watch th' sunset. Been awhile, an' I dunno when I'll next git th' chance."

She drew in a breath that would have almost certainly started an argument, but then Darnoth caught her eye and shook his head minutely. *Let him do this,* he tried to convey with his expression. *For me. Please.*

Drawing in a deep breath, Riella huffed a sigh of fond exasperation, aimed at both of them equally. "All right then," she said, moderating her tone. "We can stay just a little longer."

So they sat, with Darnoth on one side of Tal's chair and Riella on the other, and they watched as the sun set slowly over the western hills. It was a peaceful time, and Darnoth felt himself perceptibly relaxing. Between the two of them, Tal was like a graven idol, only the movement of his eyes behind barely-open lids showing that he was still awake.

As the sun dipped over the horizon, it reddened, the light illuminating the clouds above them until it seemed the whole sky was afire. A slow smile spread across Tal's aged visage, redistributing the lines as he took in the sight as if for the first time. "Never git tired o' that," he said softly. "Seen it with so many people. Gar'skoth … Losk'tareth … Miranda … Khemet … Marduk … Sasha … Rob … Eddie … Sandy … Stella … Mark … Bran …" His voice trailed off.

"Uncle Tal?" asked Riella, her voice hesitant. Darnoth looked across at her in the dying light and registered almost with a shock that she was his age, that his greying temples were reflected in her own hair. They'd been mere infants in arms when Uncle Tal had awoken from his billion-year stasis, and he'd been a part of their lives ever since. Tal had tutored her in the basics of medicine and healing before she'd gone on to more formal training, just as he'd taught Darnoth and his fellows how to construct a good hunting bow and spear and how to use both in the field. "Can I ask you a question?"

"Go ahead." Tal's eyes didn't shift from the glory of the sunset. "Ain't like I got any secrets worth keepin' anymore."

Riella leaned against his chair and he put his hand on her shoulder, letting her rest her head against his bicep. "Was it worth it? Your long life, I mean. Would you change any of it?"

He didn't answer at first, breathing deeply of the evening air under the burning sky. "Yeah, it was worth it," he said eventually. "There was times when I wasn't sure that I was doin' th' right thing, but it all turned out good in the end. I wouldn't change a single damn part of it."

"Good," she said. "I'm glad."

Silence fell again as the sun slid below the horizon. The light painting the clouds above lessened in hue, then drained away altogether.

As the shadows marched across the land, Uncle Tal spoke again. "Y'hear that?" His voice was dreamy, as though he was almost asleep. Darnoth suppressed a question; he was sure Tal wasn't speaking to him anyway. "Th' mammoth. They're on th' move … it'll be a good hunt, this season." His voice died away, leaving the whisper of the wind as the only sound on the hilltop.

Darnoth knew what mammoth were; or rather, what they had been. There were none left on Earth, of course. Not anymore. He made a mental note to ask the Collective if this could be remedied.

Almost inaudibly, Uncle Tal spoke one last time. These words were in the old language he had taught them all, what he called the Speech of his people. His voice was just a whisper by now, but Darnoth knew the words well enough to follow along. *This is my home, my hearth, my land and my blood. Here is where I make my stand.* These were deep words, more a binding pledge than a mere promise.

And then the last of the air left Tal's lungs, and he … ceased. Between one moment and the next, all that was left of the oldest Neandertal was his mortal shell. His existence, which had spanned a significant fraction of the life of the *universe,* had reached its inevitable end.

Riella sat up and looked around. She instinctively felt for a pulse in his wrist, then shook her head.

Darnoth just sat, feeling his eyes fill with tears. Through the immeasurable sadness, he felt a tiny ray of relief that Tal had spent the last of his life in a place of peace among his own kin, his own kind. At the end, in his own way, he'd been content.

Slowly, leaving Uncle Tal to be alone with the gathering dusk, the pair of them stood up and went down the hill to pass on the word. They would be back to take the body to prepare for the funeral, but for now he could be left alone in the place he had enjoyed.

Tal looked around then stood up in the deepening twilight, finding it easier than he had in years. "Well, that's new," he muttered. He wasn't quite sure if this was the last firing of neurons in a dying brain or something different, and it was kind of late to be asking someone.

WELL, DON'T LOOK AT ME. I DON'T DEAL WITH THAT SORT OF THING.

Turning his head, he eyed the figure that stood beside him in Darnoth's place. The details weren't easy to pin down but there was a hint of a robe, draped over what could've been a skeleton. If he squinted hard, he could make out a scythe, and perhaps an hourglass, but it was difficult to tell.

"Took your damn time," he muttered.

YOU DIDN'T EXACTLY MAKE IT EASY FOR ME, YOU KNOW.

"Wasn't aware I was obliged to." He stretched out of habit, popping his back into place before he recalled that this wasn't strictly necessary anymore. "So, where we going from here? Am I gonna see my family again?"

It turned out skeletons were really good at shrugging. **I'M JUST HERE FOR THE COLLECTION SIDE OF THINGS. WHERE YOU GO AFTER THIS IS UP TO YOU.**

"Good. Then I will." He paused. "Gotta ask. How did Gr'takk *know?* About everything?"

STILL NOT MY SIDE OF THINGS. YOU'LL HAVE TO ASK *HIM* THAT.

"About what I thought. Well, are we gonna keep wasting time, or are we goin' already?"

BUT YOU—YES, WE ARE GOING. NOW.

They walked down off the hilltop, fading as they went.

It was decided that Uncle Tal would be buried on the hilltop where he had passed. A starship, summoned by Stefan, descended almost to the hilltop and let out Bran, who was wearing the uniform of an Academy cadet. Then it rose away, hovered overhead, and lifted the entire top of the hill away with a tractor field.

By contrast, Darnoth and willing volunteers from all Nine Villages dug a hole beneath with hand tools that had been old when Uncle Tal was a boy. Hand-carved slabs, long prepared in anticipation of this day, were likewise lifted over by tractor beam and guided into place by Darnoth himself. These fitted together into a stone tomb, which was then lined with the softest of furs before Tal himself was laid to rest within.

In Tal's right hand, Darnoth folded the flint knife he'd been holding when they released him from stasis; in his left, the first food bowl he'd taught Darnoth how to carve. The members of the Nine Villages came then, trekking over the miles separating them from the First Village, to attend the funeral of their oldest member, their sole progenitor.

If each and every one of them had left an offering, the gravesite would have been piled higher than the original hilltop. But each Village instead brought something, a masterwork of the crafts Uncle Tal had passed on to them in his years of teaching. A hunting spear, a bow, a fishing net, beautiful wooden and sandstone sculptures. Those who brought no other offering each dropped a handful of flower petals into the grave as they passed by, bidding Uncle Tal goodbye for the last time.

As the last Villager left a handful of petals—the grave was almost overflowing with them by now—Darnoth took to the wooden wheeled chair with an axe. The anguish and pain he felt lessened a little at each blow as the wood splintered and shattered. When he felt it was in enough pieces, he placed the detritus into the grave at Tal's feet. *He would've wanted it that way.*

The last slab of stone lowered on top, sealing the mortal remains of Tal within the grave, then the entire hillside settled down above it. As the starship took a higher station above the hill, as an honor guard, Darnoth and the other men lugged one last stone to the top of the hill. This time, they did it without the assistance of tractor beams. He had worked hard all night to finish the inscription, but he did not begrudge the time it had taken him.

The stone fitted neatly into a shallow depression between the two seats, precisely where the chair had been placed. On its face, it read:

UNCLE TAL
FATHER OF THE NINE VILLAGES
THE LAST OF HIS KIND
THE FIRST OF OURS
WITHOUT HIM, WE WOULD NOT BE
MAY HIS STORY NEVER BE LOST

Beneath that inscription was the pictogram that Tal had once used to designate his own name, long ago. And below that were the words that he had uttered on the hilltop before breathing his last.

This is my home, my hearth, my land and my blood.
Here is where I make my stand.

As the men stepped back from placing the stone, Stefan moved forward. He alone of those who had attended this day was not Neandertal, not one of the Nine Villages. Except that today, he was.

Taking a small silvery object from his pocket, he knelt beside the stone and dug with his bare hands in the ground, getting his hands dirty and grit under his nails. Darnoth watched, unsure what he was doing, but knowing that this was something he had to do.

When Stefan judged the hole deep enough, he took the silvery object and buried it in the hole, then covered it over. Climbing to his feet, he looked at his hands, tried to dust them off, then wiped them on his trousers, to little real effect. Shrugging as if to say, *what can I do about that now*, he walked back to where Darnoth stood.

And then, just as Darnoth's curiosity was about to make him ask anyway, a hologram flickered into life next to the stone. It was a transparent but otherwise perfect likeness of Uncle Tal, standing next to the stone and leaning on his stick. Looking out over the Nine Villages with a slight smile on his face.

No, Darnoth decided. *Watching* over them.

"Thank you," he said to Stefan. "That's … good. Really good. I think he'd like that."

"He'd complain about it," Stefan said with a quirk of a smile, though tears glinted in his eyes. Darnoth had them in his own eyes, so he couldn't judge.

"As I said." Darnoth smiled despite himself. "He'd like it." He turned to Bran. "How long are you back for?"

"I have a two-day leave," his son reported. He looked up and waved. The starship dipped its bow once, as if in respect, then vanished skyward.

"Good." At times like this, family needed to be together. "Come along. We have a wake to attend. You too, Stefan. We'll find someplace for you to wash your hands."

As they descended the hill, Stefan's rueful laughter trailed behind them. And on the hilltop, Uncle Tal stood and watched them go.

—**End**—

Acknowledgements

I want to thank Karen (Angel466) for her tireless work in beta-reading my writing, even when it's not something she would willingly read for fun.

Likewise, I want to thank the anonymous people who put forth the appropriate prompts on Reddit, that ended up giving rise to this book.

I also want to pre-emptively thank everyone who buys and reads this book.

You're all awesome.

www.ingramcontent.com/pod-product-compliance
Lightning Source LLC
Chambersburg PA
CBHW070405200726
48294CB00003B/1096